THE
ETIQUETTE
OF
BOOBY TRAPS

THE
ETIQUETTE
OF
BOOBY TRAPS

(A Gathering of Stories)

John Boden

CEMETERY DANCE PUBLICATIONS

Baltimore
2024

Cemetery Dance Publications
132B Industry Lane, Unit #7
Forest Hill, MD 21050
www.cemeterydance.com

Trade Paperback Edition

ISBN:
978-1-58767-988-9

Cover Artwork and Design © 2024 by Matthew Revert
Interior Design © 2024 by Desert Isle Design, LLC

CONTENTS:

An Introduction *by Aaron Dries* —— 9

Come Tomorrow —— 15

Of Debris And Duty —— 25

The Recluse —— 29

The Final Kick —— 33

The Worm Eaters —— 41

Halfway Wrong Don't Make It Alright —— 43

Salten —— 55

Night Games —— 59

The Claim —— 63

In The Morning —— 79

Doodlebug —— 81

Them Iron Eyes Cody Blues —— 95

Cottonmouth —— 99

The Going Rate —— 105

Down By The Ocean —— 109

A Fee For Fables —— 113

Intruder —— 119

The Pass —— 125

This Twilight Garden —— 129

Summer Gullet —— 131

Tinsel —— 137

For Ken Wood (K. Allen Wood)
for getting it started.

AN INTRODUCTION;

OR HOW I LEARNED TO STOP WORRYING AND LOVE THE NOW

This book is not safe. Safe in the sense of secure, reliant—something *sound*. It isn't a solid experience. It turned to taffy when I was done with it, a sticky mess my hands pushed through. Me and it, becoming one.

It would be easy, I guess, to tell you in an 'introduction', what to expect from the book ahead (the one in your hands now). However, I think it is better to simply describe how I feel, and what is left of me now that the last page has been turned.

John Boden's words are on my fingers. I'm not going to lie—it makes me panic a little. So, I find myself rubbing my palms on my trousers, only to stain those, too. Nervously tug at my hair. Sentences and paragraphs among the wiry grey and auburn strands, as I'm trying to get myself clean, feeling age tug at my elbows, dragging me closer to the carpet in my living room where I finished The *Etiquette of Boobytraps* on my back, a pillow under my head. This book.

Your fingers are now pressing against these pages, on this screen. And I'm telling you, *telling you* not warning you, that what happened to me will also happen to you.

It's okay to be a bit uncertain, even a bit sad. But it can't be stopped. It has already begun. The alchemy, its spell. This collection of stories has already started to meld with your body and mind, pushing through one another, mixing into one big lumpy hot pot of emotional gumbo. It isn't just the book in your hair, in the corner of your eyes, under your fingertips, in your fingernails. It is who *I* used to be, my hands, my hair, even the clothes I'm wearing are in the book, and are now in your life and living as one. Our atoms have become indivisible.

They always were.

Because when John Boden writes about himself, about his characters, he's writing about you. Me. Us. We just didn't know it at the start.

This is his gift.

So, here is my advice:

Don't resist.

Yes, meld.

This process is a kind of hello. A kind of hug. John creates stories that frighten and startle because they are so imbued with the vibrancy of life, just as *you* are imbued with life, which only serves to remind you of the bones beneath your skin, that we're all just flesh. And all flesh rots. We don't live forever. We can only hope to do well with the deals we're dealt. Let the melt happen, let your fingers mix with the page. Your tattoos are its tattoos. You are each each other's spine, bone-against bone in a kind of helix, unifying. This is the great pleasure only a great book can bring.

John Boden. This feeling is his doing.

We're in the soul gumbo now, you and me and John and everyone we know, simmering in memory and mind okra and nerves and paper and so many wonderful words.

I FINISHED READING *The Etiquette of Bobby Traps*, tales ranging from flash to shorts, absurd observations to knock-outs delivered with a master touch, grief parables to laconic bewitchments, and decided, gosh, I really need a walk. A bit of post-mind warp decompression. My brother's dogs are staying with us. They come along. Off leash through the bush, the bigger dog running after a kangaroo as if he knows that he'll do with it if he catches it, the smaller dog lumbering behind and panting like a fury mirror image of myself. Branches whip my face. Sticks whip my shins. It smells as if it might rain. There are two eucalyptus trees on my left, stately ghosts rubbing their limbs together the way flies do before they drink vomit. This scratching sound, kind of squeaky, wriggles into my ears. It reminds me of someone crying, that sound. I am, without warning, aware that I'm walking through an ecosystem. I look down. Ants everywhere. Their purpose, their tiny missions, whilst alien to me, poke at my emotions. Another look at the trees reveals that they are barked with tongues.

It is then I realise I have been well-and-truly John Bodened.

After reading *The Etiquette of Boobytraps*, and being caught in the consequential web of its magic, in the stickiness of it all, I am aware now that I never exist solely. I never really did. I have always been surrounded by the missions of others, of things I don't understand, things stronger than me, surrounded by memories made manifest, of anxieties grown concrete, watched by spirits that haunt me in wonderful and frightening ways, ghosts that whisper at me to turn right and not left or to turn back because it's not just rain in my immediate future ... but thunder.

And lightning.

Danger ahead.

Sometimes, a book is not just a book. Reading is never the solitary experience people think it is. It's a commune of a kind. And you want this. We all hunger for it, right? On the other side of Planet Earth, John Boden is at his desk and taking from this same ephemeral place, words that are plucked with utter precision. And now, all the way down here on my living room floor with that pillow under my head, those words were read by me as they are about to be read by you, and I can feel me saying Y-E-S to a world that was always there. Yet only the very special can see. And only the very talented can unearth.

John Boden is one of those very special, very talented humans. He is not just a storyteller. He is one of our great illuminators.

I HAVE COME home. There was rain, after all. The whole house shivers in the wind. Thunder makes the windows rattle. I've unplugged my laptop because I still have that fear that lightning will strike the house and travel through the wires and come up through the computer like a blinding Jack-In-The-Box and fry the eyes out of my head. The dogs look at me with a kind of befuddlement—looks that say:

How could the world we were just exploring become ... *this*? *And so quickly?*

I go over to them and give them a hug. There are images in my head, a cloudy, itchy, familiar, foreign, intoxicating cloud. Some of these images are from my work, from my past, from an imagined future, and they have been kicked into life by John's book. I'm wondering if there will be a voice from a fish in a pond and if what it is saying is about John or his characters of the creature's truths are for me. I'm wondering if my hurts are its hurts and our hurts are your hurts—or will be. I guess what I'm describing, or trying to describe, is a kind of transcendence. Yes, that's it. John Boden's *The Etiquette of Boobytraps* is a transcendent experience.

But you have to want to go there. You must be ready.

Are you ready?

Are you willing to look inwards? That's what this book demands. Be brave. Be strong. To look inwards is a way out. Writing as good as this is freedom. For that, I say thank you, John. Because, to be honest, it's been a rough couple of years over here in my world—and it's left me a bit weary, jaded, and seeking the ugly in far too much. You have led me (as he'll lead you) through intimate stories of anguish and pain and hilarity and weirdness and folksy brilliance to *here*, this exact spot, in this exact moment in time. And I'm feeling so different, changed. I'm with my brother's dogs and it is raining outside, and it's just so fucking beautiful. I don't think I could see that before, what was always there. I can now.

—— —— ——

BUT I'M WONDERING how long this feeling can—*will*—last.

Surely, you can only feel this alive for so long.

Aaron Dries, July 2024

COME TOMORROW

"If we'd had a dime for every year we got with our little Amy, we'd have a dollar. One measly dollar! That's what my little girl's time here would be...not enough for a fuckin' candy bar!"

His voice was almost sputtering as it came out in heaves.

Steve's face was boiled red, the sheen of tears from eyes to nose to chin gave him a high gloss. His eyes were nearly rolled over white like an attacking shark. The stern but soft presence of Mel's hand on his shoulder was the only thing keeping him from grabbing that doctor by the throat and squeezing until the man's eyes dulled.

"Mister Brody..."

The young man in the white coat paused as he carefully tried to sew together comforting words for this couple and had as much success as trying to carry water in a sieve.

The bigger man held up a hand, one finger pointed to the ceiling.

"You told us by the time the end came she'd be comfortable. You told us it would be peaceful, that she'd just go to sleep and not wake again, or she'd be so weary she'd just close her eyes."

15

Steve's grimace of grief faltered into a deep sneer. It rose in the corner to show a glimpse of stained teeth.

"You were wrong!"

He sobbed, and the roar filled the small room. The young doctor hung his head, and Mel kept her hand on her husband's shoulder, the chain that held back the beast. Her tears flowed freely but quietly.

"You know what it was like? I mean, you fucking ought to, you stood right there. Right! Goddamn! There! You watched us hold our little girl's hands and try to calm her while she panicked. While she fought to breathe. Fought to stay here. She *knew* what was coming and it terrified her. Her eyes darted. Her breath came so fast. She knew, and she tried to be calm, but she was ten. Ten! How calm can a kid be when it's time to go?"

His rant was petering out. His strength was bleeding from him like he was a gut shot deer. He looked at his shoes and then leveled a gaze at the doctor. His clean-shaven face looked scalded, his cheeks wet. Steve knew it wasn't the young man's fault. Wasn't the fault of anyone really. Maybe God's. He drew a loud and deep breath and cried some more, spinning around and into the arms of his wife. They cocooned one another in their grief, and the young doctor left them alone to do it.

CAN YOU OVERDOSE *on antacids?*

Even his inner voice was rusted from disuse.

Steve's stomach was burning. It had been since Christmas. He closed his eyes and felt it - raw and paper-cut-scalding. He envisioned a lifetime of words he'd held back and swallowed. The verbal stillborn slowly digesting in thick belly fluids like dinosaurs in a tar pit. The sharp elbows of letters like M and L and V gouging and tearing tissues to remind him that words can be forever - even those never spoken. The only ghosts that cannot be exorcized. He looked at the pile of bills on the hall table. An offensive offering at the foot of the picture of his dear Mel. He slid them onto the floor and kicked them under the bookshelf. He palmed two more tablets, chewed them with aching teeth. Outside, the sky stumbled, and it began to rain.

IT'S ONLY BEEN two years, but every minute of every day of every single month of them has been itching with an aching. That longing to hear their voices bouncing off of the windows like trapped moths. To see their faces - smiling or, hell, I'd even take angry or crying, just to see them - would be the greatest gift of all. I'd relive a thousand fights with Melanie or fifty times as many fits with little Amy if it meant I got to hear them again. Why didn't you just take 'em both together somehow, Lord? Maybe Amy wouldn't have been so scared.

Steve flushed the toilet and looked at the haggard old man in the mirror. The man was made of old thin paper and stubble. More wrinkled than anything with welts for eyes that blew reddened kisses at him through his reflection.

One is the loneliest number. It's barely a number at all. It's just a line.

I got Mel for almost a year and a half after Amy. Long enough to almost start to feel normal again. As normal as you can feel after you bury your daughter.

STEVE SAT ON the edge of the bed and looked at the closet door hanging open like a mouth. The hanging shirts, the mounds of dirty pants and socks filling it, and his gaze settled on the fishing rod that leaned against the back wall.

Maybe that's just what I need to do...go sit by the water and not think. Just be at rest. Just occupy space.

He raked fingers through greasy hair and stood up. Bones crackled like a summer bonfire. He dressed and grabbed the pole from the closet. It had a thin coat of dust on it from the years it hibernated behind wedding dress shirts and funeral slacks. He hunkered and brushed away socks and underwear until he saw the orange plastic of the tackle box. He grabbed it gently like a treasure chest and opened it. Hooks and sinkers and jiggers and flies. Scissors and Band-Aids and extra spools of line. No frills. He almost smiled as he closed it and hefted it onto the bed. His mind swam back to the last time he had been fishing. Amy was all of four years old, and patience was just a string of letters she couldn't pronounce.

Steve stepped into the boots at the foot of the bed and, with his gear, left the house as empty as it was when he was in it.

THE SUN WAS barely up when Steve slowed the truck and parked in the loose stones at the end of the bridge. The NO PARKING sign that lived there had been knocked down by plows during the winter and lay beneath dirt and debris. Steve stepped over it without a thought and walked to where the railing began, at the start of the bridge.

He managed to fold himself low enough to get beneath the side rail and scooched down the hill to the fallen pillar that edged the water. The cement was cold through the denim of his jeans. He popped the lid of the box and rummaged for a decent lure, gently pushing aside sinkers and rubber worms, but stopping when his fingers happened upon the hair tie. Hot pink and stretchy fabric. He gently held it to his face and inhaled. It held the faintest trace of Amy's scent-soap and strawberry shampoo. He even thought he could feel a strand of her pale hair on his upper lip. That lip raised into a smile as his eyes shed water.

"Let's go fishing, little girl," he mumbled as he tied the pink elastic to the line about an inch above the hook. He knotted the sinker and worked a faux purple worm onto the barb. He leaned sideways to cast and watched the worm land in a pool out near the drop. He sat still and sang softly to himself. The smile stayed on his lips like a scar.

You'll never know dear...how much I love you...

He stopped singing when the line jerked, and he heard the splashing.

--- --- ---

THE FISH WAS small, and its scales shone pink in the morning sun, even beneath the murk of the water. Steve reeled slowly, and the fish barely fought him once it was out of the water. Its brilliance was dazzling - a prism of pinks and purples as the day's light met it. It reminded him of the pink sequins on Amy's school bag. He reached out with a shaking hand and gripped the fish, finding its flesh to be damp but not slippery. He squeezed slightly and popped the barb free of its pulsating lip. Its blue eyes never left his face. Steve stared and brought the fish closer to his nose, nearly touching it.

"*Daddy.*"

A shiver scurried down his spine, and he squeezed the fish a little tighter out of surprise. Its mouth opened wider, and a wheezing sound escaped it. He tilted his ear closer to that gaping mouth and held the fish close again.

"*Daddy,*" — croaked the small voice — "*Throw me back.*"

Steve dropped the fish into the shallows at his feet and watched it swim away. A pink blur beneath the surface. It swam right to dark waters where it dropped deeper.

"You're off your nut, fella. That fish did not call you Daddy."

Unless it did, and you knew that voice...

He looked at the line at his feet and realized the hair tie was no longer fastened to it. He hooked another worm and cast his line again. It sat, ignored, for nearly an hour before the sky grew dark as storm clouds began to appear. Steve packed up to leave before the sky broke open. He heard splashing out near the deep hole, but he didn't look to see what it was.

————

SLEEP THAT NIGHT was no more than a few troubled slats of tossing and turning with eyes closed but his brain running full speed. When the sun worked its feeble fingers through the dirty blinds of his room, Steve groaned. He finally wrestled himself into a sitting position and saw the pole leaning against the dresser where he'd put it. He frowned and pulled on the same jeans he'd worn a day earlier and grabbed the pole.

He stopped in the room that was once his daughter's and, from the dresser top, scooped another hair tie and a bead bracelet she had made in Bible school. He stowed them in his shirt pocket and headed for the door. He paused by the hall table and looked at the picture of Mel. He stared at that beautiful face he had kissed a thousand times and loved more than anything. He propped the pole against the bookshelf and pulled out the drawer in the table and removed the item he sought. He headed for the river.

─ ─ ─

THE WATER WAS high and moving fast. The air felt heavy with humidity even after a night of storms. Steve closed the trunk of the car and slung his hip waders over his shoulder while he picked up the rod and tackle box. He maneuvered down the bank to his spot on the pillar. The water's edge was almost to the base of it and about a foot and a half higher than yesterday. Steve tied on an extra sinker and pulled the bright yellow tie from his pocket. He wrapped it around the hook and cast his line.

Within minutes there was a tug, followed by another. Steve gave a quick yank and began reeling in his catch. The fish was similar to the previous day's - a bright yellow this time - and the eyes were deep blue and enormous. He leaned to grip the fish and held it up to his face. The eyes were familiar to him. His breath hitched, and he worked the hook free from the fish's lip.

"Daddy."

Steve held it and looked at the creature in his hand. It did not squirm but remained still, mouth opening and closing. Eyes never leaving him.

"Daddy."

"This cannot be happening."

Steve knelt and held the fish to the water. It began to move frantically just before he released his grip. Before its mouth disappeared beneath the surface, he swore he heard it say, *"I love you."*

─ ─ ─

21

HE SAT ON the pillar and just stared at the water for the rest of the day. As the world turned, and the sun moved, the shadows huddled in different spots on the water. The deep hole never got any light. The arms of the trees that were towering above it saw to that. Steve considered that he was losing his mind. That the last two years had eroded what sanity he had originally possessed. Losing Amy and then Mel had simply broken an already cracked windshield. He sat and watched the shadowed depths out near the middle of the river. His brow furrowed as he dug a hand into his pocket. He looked at the plastic strip lying across his palm. The white paper encased within it. The name **Melanie Brody** typed in simple font, followed by a patient number, and then three letters he had hoped to never see again: D.O.A.

Steve picked up the fishing pole and tied the cut bracelet around the hook. He breathed deeply and looked at the fading sun as he cast the line. It landed with a plop out in the deep.

He sat and watched the sun slowly set, and when the horizon appeared to be bleeding, a minute or two later, something took the bait.

Steve did not reel the line but instead leaned the pole against the concrete while he put on his wading boots. The line stayed taut as he began walking into the water. He slowed when he felt himself nearing the drop, felt his toes lose purchase on the soft ground beneath. He stopped and slowly began reeling in something pale beneath the water. Something large. He felt flushed as he gripped the line with his left hand and slowly pulled toward him, leaning and pushing his right hand under the surface. He waved it back and forth.

It was dark under the canopy of branches, and he caught a flash of under the water's muddy cowl and was about to pull back when he felt the hand grasp his.

Five cold fingers wrapped themselves around his hand. He was not pulled, the hand just held his.

He traced his index finger over the holding hand and felt the band on the ring finger he had traced hundreds of times, both awake and in slumber. He laughed, but it was a barking sound in the quiet dusk.

"Mel?" He croaked.

The hand pulled slightly and then released its grip on his. He heard a rush of water and a splash out in the darkness.

Steve stood there.

Cold water up to his waist, in growing dark, he smiled while he cried.

— — —

THE SUN WAS just starting to poke a timid tongue through the loose lips of the morning. Steve stood by the river and watched the sun stick its nose over the mountain. He smelled the cool water rushing by. Breathed the odor of wet leaves and silt the river carried. He smiled and bent to pick up a stone. He picked up several more. He filled all of the pockets of his cargo pants with them. He slowly walked to the pillar and picked up the length of rope he'd placed there - one end tied to a cinder block. He looped it around his neck and picked up the brick, cradling it like a newborn. He heard a splash out near the deep and smiled in that direction.

He took out his wallet and laid it on the pillar next to his tackle box and rod. He took furtive steps into the water and did not falter as he made his way to the shadows.

He had a reunion to get to.

OF DEBRIS AND DUTY

The thin fingers of light that made it through the blinds were arthritic at best, barely illuminating the man in the stained uniform as he looked at the items spread across the desk. His desk.

—*A bent and rusty sheriff's badge.*

Hetrick stared out the dirty window at the armed men who stormed down the streets, the marching cadence of their boots on cracked concrete like thunder and drums. The carpet of bones and glass and blood, muffling nothing.

—*A doll's leg.*

The smoke choked the skies, the sun sizzled like a bloody yolk overhead. Crows and vultures danced around it, their screeches blending with the screams from the ground. All shrouded by towers of angry flame. Hoarse shouts and prayers fluttered around like mosquitoes.

—*A broken toy bus.*

Hetrick looked at his wrist, at the pale band around the skin where a watch had lived. He had no need to mark the passage of time anymore. No one really did. He stared at the spot where arm turned to hand, at the blue vein that lived beneath the skin, and wondered how long it would take him to work up the nerve to open it.

—*A scissor blade.*

He was glad his wife wasn't here to see what was going on. What had happened to the world? There was nothing left but his job, and even that was up for debate — one with only one side. He swiveled in his chair as he heard the tanks approach. Heard the firecracker popping of skulls beneath their tread. He pinched the bridge of his nose hard enough to make his eyes water. He tasted salt at the back of his throat. He stopped spinning in his chair and stared at the cellar door, and the desk that was pushed against it. He still heard the noises down there, furtive and vermin. He hoped.

—*A balsa wood plane with a broken wing.*

He pulled back the curtain and watched the soldiers shoot the children. Watched the children shatter and fall. Watched the ones who got away stab and bite and claw. Saw an old man take a dive from the church tower, the bell rope tied in a large knot around his stubbled neck. A faded Christmas bow on a swinging present. Watched as a woman stepped in front of the tank, baby in her arms. She held it out as an offering, her smile broad and strong as she went down. There was singing and laughter swaddled in screams and howling. Layers and layers.

—*A buffalo nickel.*

His hands over his unshaven face, his eyes closed. He was still and listened to the insanity outside. To the buzzing from the corners of the room, corners where the blood pooled. Where the deputy and secretary fed the flies. Underneath it all, he heard a small voice. His own. From twenty years ago. "R-E-D spells red and you are not it..." His tears trailed down dirty arms and onto the desk and the items spread upon it.

—*A yellow super ball.*

Hetrick looked at all of these things spread on the blotter. These toys and remnants of childhood meant nothing anymore. Almost biblical in their accusations. The phone was a corpse beneath dust and dead moths. A pencil and some old bills decorated the perimeter of the desk surface, the pale green blotter was a show stage. The artifacts of youth, of the days before he was an adult. An entire history from — there was a thump and the sound of breaking glass from below.

—*A bent bottle cap.*

From, was it really only a week ago? Hetrick looked at his name on the frosted glass of the other door. Backwards, his name. He used to be the law once. That was kind of backwards too.

—*A cracked leather coin purse with a wedding ring inside.*

Hetrick looked out the window once more. A group of children had surrounded a young soldier and were nailing her to the church door. Banging serrated kitchen knives through her wrists with bricks and an old boot. A blond boy pierced her side with a broken piece of wood. She was screaming and there was no sound. The smoke made it surreal — shadows and stealth, spidery movement, and jagged shifts. When he saw the little girl with eyes like his and a matching dimple in her chin, the same little girl holding the tangled crown of barbed wire and string, he sighed and shook his head. He picked up an item from the desk and took a step towards the door, sliding his boots so as to not make a sound. Something heavy banged against the cellar door. Wet laughter scurried from the crack beneath it like roaches.

He sniffed and drew a deep breath, which he held hostage. He closed his eyes and mumbled—

"These are my youth and they have starved." The metal on his tongue was rainwater bitter.

—*A loaded service pistol is a skeleton key.*

THE RECLUSE

She types with her head down, bowing like a monk. The pallid glow from the monitor paints her face white. She is a china doll. Her fingers dance - *clickity-click* - over the keys. Information flutters invisibly through the air over our heads. I watch her and listen and silently swoon. The air kicks on and makes the calendars and notes taped to cubicle walls flutter and whisper like leaves in a slight breeze. The ductwork sighs cool.

—The girl has been gone for at least an hour. I sit there and stare at my computer. The cursor blinking at me, cussing and degrading my lack of "*Pussy*," it taunts, "*You could have gone to her, walked right up to her and spoken.*" Guilty as I had not. I chew another hangnail and suck the blood and sigh. The cursor keeps baiting me. "Fuck you," I sneer as I turn it off. I pinch the bridge of my nose until spots dance before my tired eyes. A tear of sweat rolls down my forehead.

—I go to her cube and sit in her chair. I touch her pens and pencils. I smell her box of tissues and smile at the candid pictures of her and her friends. Her stupid cat. Washed out comic strips taped to the wall panel. I had almost forgotten about Ziggy. My chest feels as though it could explode at any second. My sternum creaks, as though all the feelings I have for her will break free. And if that happens, all the ugliness I've held inside would seek liberation as well. Thick, squirming tendrils of bile black and seething rage. Disdain and disgust dripping from the tips of twitching tentacles. I lay my glasses on her desk, perspiration trickling from black plastic and staining the blotter. I rub my aching head. My stomach grumbles and sends an urgent burn up the back of my throat. This is love.

—The following day, she comes in early. I am at my desk, actually I never left. I washed myself in the restroom sink and put on a spare shirt that I keep in my desk. The wrinkles hide behind the pinstripes. She smiles as she walks by, and something cracks below my breastbone. I look at her and smile back. "Hi," I attempt, but the feeble thing gets lost in the air, a mote of dust in a storm. She goes down the row and disappears behind her wall. I roll my chair to the desk and turn on the monitor. Cursor says "Good morning, coward," and I flick it off. My fingers ache, so I stretch and flex them. They crackle like flames. "Do it," I goad myself. I get up and walk the row like a condemned man.

—"Emily," I say as I turn the corner. She turns smiling, and I smile and raise the hand that holds the string. The invisible string that holds back the myriad. All the love and hate. All the anger and awe. All the seedy inner workings. She sees it is me, and the smile falters. A little, but enough to break the string. Deep inside there is a snap and a growl. A snarl that swells and grows, and I feel suddenly tight. This is how it always plays out for me. Always. Déjà vu and lazy eight.

—I cry as I unbutton my shirt and barely get it off before the maw gnashes and barks. The saliva foams. The tongues waggle and pull her in. A hundred and seventeen teeth grind and eradicate. She is devoured, and I am alone. I stand statue-still for minutes that seem like days. Slowly, I button the shirt and look around at her cubicle. The clock says it is nearly seven. I have a few minutes to clean up and get to my desk before anyone else shows up. I will sit quietly all morning. Hope no one notices Emily's void. No one notices anything different. No one notices me. Just like any other day.

—Maybe the next girl will be the one, maybe I can just say "hello."

THE FINAL KICK

I.

Virginia Beach, VA

The ocean is a womb = water + salt.
A thousand men line the beach, to spill their seed into a churn-
ing sea.
Onto the surf where it glistens like pearls by dawn's early light.
Behind them is another army.
– and behind them, another.
– and another.
Pumping fists and squinting eyes, flinging the future in sticky globs.
The waves take it like the mouth of a whore, with a roaring smile,
miles long and wide.
Pregnant with promises and deceptions.
The ocean is a womb.

II.

Ishwick, NJ (also everywhere in the world)

The flicker boxes in the shop windows glower and scream
and shriek and stare. Filled with faces and fashions and fear.

Defecating static destruction built from vowels and consonants.

Words are sharpened like the beaks of birds.

Hooked like thumbnail or curved like tongue.

Rubbed against stone and skull—

—until we can make them stick, until we can drive them in.

Truth is the most comfortable of clubs when held in a righteous fist, even more so when it's a lie.

The crowds walk by and ignore these displays. They build landscapes behind their eyes with the fragments they glean.

Shreds of opinion and slivers of conjecture. Fronds of fact and the rubble of ruminations. Everything that aligns them also tears them apart.

They are razors made of rubber.

They build walls inside.

Their souls squirm and dub themselves *Fortunato*.

The world throbs and oozes—

A wound on an axis.

III.

Dunkenny, NM

The sunshine in her eyes and heart pull her from sleep like a dried bandage from a stubborn laceration.

The whispers tunnel through her bones like microscopic miners.

Her jaw feels hollow and heavy as lead. Waiting for a Cain to put it to good use.

Her voice is the lost art of alchemy.

Her voice is practiced in shadow and dust.

Her tongue is a mummified paw.

She lurches from the pueblo/house/hovel/trailer:

She pounces at the passersby. Sputtering passages and accolades. Hemorrhaging hymns and histrionics. Touting tutelage and torments.

Proclamations flurry around her like a blaze of hornets.

Her hands crisply clap in time with the *joy joy joy joy* down in her heart (where!).

The sky swirls slowly like dirty water around a drain.

Clouds cataract the view like peeking through gauze at a skittish wound.

That wound is your salvation, pal!

IV.

Matilde, OK

The jets are flying low and fast, with the frequency of dishonesty. Razors across the wrists of the heavens.

The voices that clot the air are clasped between flexing fists and never-make-it-to-the-important ears. The innocent stand and stare upward while the guilty gaze lower.

Children smile like kewpie dolls, cracked like old plaster and painted badly. Welcoming eyes to behold what comes next.

The word of God is slurred through broken teeth and fission.

The planes leave loping stitches across the wild blue yonder.

They will suppurate.

And it will rain down in the only baptism we deserve.

V.

Khanmo, Thailand

Along the ocean's maw, the coastal city sleeps.

The sun licks at the edges of night, darkness receding like diseased gums. The stars shiver and flee.

But—
Beneath the waves...
Beneath the swimming fish,
the floating detritus and seaweed fingers,
A fissure opens up on the floor of the sea. Red clouds of blood puff
into the brine like the breath of a fat man on a winter morning.
The saltwater embraces this.
The fish slow and die and float to the surface like carrion buoys.
The crack in the earth widens and hemorrhages more and more.
The sides of the fresh chasm are lined with teeth -
A million times a million rows of hand-sized pyramids of ser-
rated bone.
They gnash and grind against one another
as the canyon spreads like a teenager's legs.
Like lies and rumors.
Like a fact presented too fucking late.
The rift emits a dull roar that shakes the coral and the buildings
on the shore.
After three minutes of this, it goes silent again.
Along the beach, all of this went noticed.
Like so many disasters do.
So many miracles as well.

VI.
Massoning, GA

The voices always scream, both inside your head and outside.
There was a time when this wasn't so. There was a speaking
voice. There was no reason. There was empathy and entropy.
There was support and sympathy.
There was "Hello, how are you?" and "I'm so sorry to hear that."

They all died in the fire. That immolation that occurred not long after we surged from the swill and grew our weak legs.

Our manners are embers, glowing in the pit.

Blossoming arms that could save but choose to strangle.

...*What are words worth when no one listens anymore*...

Isolation among millions is the hippest place.

Individuality while chanting the same fucking chant, wearing the same fucking uniform, and expecting a wholly different outcome.

This is the way we work this bitch.

Dry your tears and hand me that wrench.

VII.

Steelwater, PA

The wise man built his house upon the rock.

Rock beats scissors.

Scissors beat dead trees.

A fool makes his home upon the sand.

Sand is embryonic glass.

Houses are shadows - solid and comforting - but quickly morph to tombs and prisons.

Aluminum siding is barbed wire.

Painted brick, the unkindest of guards.

(above)

The behemoth stirs in festering slumber. It drags a long hand along a heaving side and the ragged nails rake the hair sprouting there. Graze the tumorous boil that protrudes from beneath its nipple. A glorious orb of rippled flesh that is throbbing slightly. It stings, but not enough to rouse the beast completely from its sleep.

The behemoth scratches at the blemish and smiles slightly without waking.

What is a God?
Be it a notion?
An act or movement — an unbridled emotion or unfenced
territory?
What is a God?
A monster. A man. A minus. A mystery.
What is a God?
A foundation, cracked and sinking...
A carcass, rotted and stinking...
A spine as crooked as a politician's smile...
What is a God?
(All together now boys and girls, in a strong sure voice)
Who gives a fuck...*
*a very small voice in the back: "What isn't?"

VIII.
DeFoose, IA

The sky tumults and begins to rend —
behind it something very gray and large looms.
An enormous arm through an open window
AND
be ye a builder of houses on either sand or stone.
They shall splinter beneath it just the same.
The angriest god is the one in the mirror.
The kindest god is the one who destroys everything.

IX.
Chance, MI

The sky is filled with gray flesh.
It ripples like heat from summer asphalt.

A million screams hum as it smothers them,
muffling prayers that weren't worth much more at full volume.
The sky's gone out.
The god has risen.
He has no name and no face.
He is just like me.
Just like you.
Except —
He's rising to his full potential.

X.

It is over.
There is only shadow and wriggling black.
Stars float in it like dead frogs in a poisoned pond.
Years drag into centuries.
Pregnant with histories hungry for repetition.
Unlearned lessons stick the longest.

ZZZZZZZ...

THE WORM EATERS

Lawrence watched the rains from his station underneath the carport. The clouds had literally rumbled in from nowhere, great black bison lumbering across the rainbow plain of sky. They snorted thunder and spat lightning. The sky opened and let loose a rain of maggots and worms that covered the ground in a fine, wriggling blanket. Children and emaciated adults scrambled from beneath their shelters to clamor and grab as many handfuls as they could, stuffing plastic bags and shoe boxes with living strings.

Some shoved great, gray handfuls into their slobbering, lipless mouths as they gathered. They moaned in disturbing ecstasy as they ate and cavorted in the slithering mud. In the shadows of his hiding place, Lawrence sat and watched and picked at the black sores that decorated his skinny legs. He popped them into his eager mouth like candy and, with disgust, grimaced at the worm eaters.

HALFWAY WRONG
DON'T MAKE IT ALRIGHT

Been sitting on the floor of the backseat in this station wagon for nearly two hours. The rough carpet on my knees is a comforting sting. I ain't bothered much about it no more. None of it. I still have the stupid 7-Eleven napkin I spit in crumpled in my fist. The stickiness has mostly dried. A potential population dead on brown paper. It just started to rain, I hear it on the roof. It sounds like the drums in the band room at school, when I was in school, a long while back. I push the napkin in the crevice where the backrest and the seat meet, where the seat belt comes out like a thick tongue. I push it back out of sight, like I'm hiding a body.

Mark, I think that was his name, Mike? No, yeah, Mark... Mark is long gone. I asked him if he wanted to sit in my car for a break and listen to the radio and smoke. He pushed his long bangs behind his ears and said sure, I smiled, and he smiled. And we kept smiling as we walked out the receiving dock doors and around to the side lot where I park the wagon. We smoked a Marlboro each and got the whole way through a Foghat song and two Motley Crue tunes before I was kissing him. In the middle of Tom Petty's

"Free Fallin'," he was squeezing my chest and trying to get his tongue down into my stomach. By the time the opening guitar of "Stranglehold" began, I let him stick it in my mouth. After almost a minute of him squirming, halfway giggling, it was over. No thank you, fuck you, or howdydo. Just yanked it out of my mouth like a baby's dummy. Hell, the door slammed before I had even found the napkin in the trash on the floor to spit his spunk in.

If I weren't used to it, I'd be pissed, but what's the use? I'm not smart enough for college. Not pretty enough for movies. Tits like mosquito bites and legs like sticks. I got an accommodating mouth and a sweet disposition, that's what my mama says. I mean used to say. And she wasn't entirely wrong.

But first, let me go back a ways. Set the scene as they say in the movies I ain't pretty enough to be in.

I was ten the first time I saw a man naked. He wasn't really a man. Just some scrawny fella that rode my mom nights after she got home from the bar. He lived with us for years but was hardly there. She'd stink of cigarettes and stale perfume while he'd reek of beer and sweat. He always smelled sourly sweet, like the apples that laid in the ground under the tree in the backyard, unfit to eat, but good for drawing yellow jackets.

They'd come stumbling in the trailer, loudly, around one in the morning. One of them would fall over the coffee table in front of the couch. The other would be giggling about it. They'd switch roles off and on, but the action was always to script. I'd lay in my bed in the little room by the bathroom, eyes squeezed shut so tight I saw blobby spots of color floating around when I opened them. I'd listen to him empty his bladder behind the wall that held my *Care Bears* poster. He'd cough and spit before he flushed, then I'd close my eyes again, listen to him leave the bathroom, and walk back the hall to their bedroom, hoping the steps continued past my door. Hoping that it wouldn't be one of the nights where they stalled and lingered. Where his heavy, wheezing breaths would scurry under the door like mice. When a small sliver of light would slice the darkness like a fresh razor as the door slowly opened with a haunted house squeak.

"Hey Dollypop, you awake. Buddy missed you, he wants to say nighty night and give you a kiss," his bar hoarse voice whispered louder than he thought. I'd stay quiet as church and pretend I was asleep. Even when the bed sunk, and the springs groaned under his weight. Even as his bark-rough hand found my leg and patted the fat part above my knee before moving upward. Even as I felt his whiskers on my chin and his thick breath on my cheeks. When I'd hear the wet slurp of him wetting his fingers in his mouth. I stayed still. I stayed quiet.

I was a brave girl. I never screamed. Not once.

Anyway, it was him I saw naked, and I don't understand the fuss over a man's prick. Looks like a shaved hamster without no legs, just small and frightened. He never put it in me, he just pulled at it while he'd rub me with his hands or work a finger in me. Pull at it until it spat stuff on my legs. He'd take the gunk on his finger and wipe it on my lips and laugh. It smelled, but I didn't fight, it meant he was done and would be out of my room directly.

I told my Mimma about when I was out there stayin' one weekend. She was my daddy's mother, and after he left for a carton of milk one day and never came back, she was around more. Took me away from Mama and Buddy. Lots more, after I told her about Buddy's nighttime visits. Mimma was old... looked like one of those dolls where the head is made out of an apple, all brown and shriveled. Smelling of sweet spice.

"Bad is bad and good is best. Them spaces between is just empty. No halfway wrongs and no nearly rights. Buddy ain't fucked you flat out but he's done as much as so. Fer cryin' out loud, Lyla, you're just a little girl. What kinda man wants to dip it in that? A sick one. An' your Mimma's gonna teach you how to fix it to right."

I stayed that whole week, and she showed me how to make the dolls, Feejees, she called 'em, I think. She said they didn't need to really look like the person, it was what we put in the body that made 'em work. She made one to show me. It was a fat ball of faded flannel, roughly stitched with green yarn and had four clothespins clipped to the seam folds that resembled sorta arms and legs. She told me it was the old man who lived in the shack across the lane from her. He was a miserable bastard, drank all day and night, and only came outside to piss off the end of the porch and kick the scrawny dog he kept chained to the tree in front. The dog-kicking was what got him in Mimma's craw, I'm sure.

"I'd like to see that dog bite his pecker off just one time, boy," she'd mutter every time the sound of his screen door banging shut floated across

the lane. She'd laugh herself to a fit of hoarse coughing that usually ended in a stained Kleenex disappearing back into her sleeve.

She sent me over after dark, after she was sure he was passed out on the couch with the TV blaring. I knew what I was to find and bring to her, so I did as I was asked.

The next two weekends, I never saw him at all. He stayed inside, and I figured he must've finally realized he had a toilet in there. But the third weekend, we saw him shamble outside, and I musta made a noise because Mimma just chuckled.

"Sins is hungry things, Lyla. The badder they are, the bigger the bites they take. But they usually swim inside and get their fill when a person is lashing out or doin' even worse things. What we done here, pet, what we done was we dropped the leash and let 'em all loose. A sin unbridled is a dog with sharper teeth, for sure. And it will just eat from inside until there ain't much a nothin' left. A guilty man will do it to himself, but a lot of bastards don't know guilt from the Queen of England, so we help 'em out. Someone has to hold the magnifying' glass sometimes."

I turned my attention back to the scene across the dirt road.

He was thin and looked like a skeleton wrapped with old butcher paper. Places where the bones were sharp, the skin looked pink and ready to bust. He was dotted with red sores, and even from my spot on the porch, I could see them oozing yellow. He stood on the end of the porch and worked his dick out of the flap of his boxers and let a stream of piss go that barely cleared his feet. It was dark, and when it hit the sun-faded pale wood of the side of the shack, it stained it red as barn paint. He didn't even bother pushing himself back in, just turned and staggered in the door. The poor mutt looked at the porch and whimpered, seemed sad there was to be no kicking, I guess even bad attention is better than none at all to the ignored.

I called Mimma that next Thursday, and she said she thought Old Man Bickle was finally dead. Said the old dog just howled and howled for almost two days straight. She took it food and water and it just kept yowling. She said she crept onto the porch and tried to peek in his filthy window, but it was covered in buzzing black flies. She opened the door enough to catch the stink and then went an' untied the dog and let it in the house before she pulled the door closed and walked back over to her trailer.

She said she waited another day and a half before she called the police, give the mutt enough time to add insult to injury. Being eaten by the dog you kicked every day for so long was the cherry on top, she said before she laughed herself coughing.

So, Buddy died when I was soon to begin eleventh grade. By the end of summer that year, he was whittled down to nothing by cancer, and while my mama sat in the living room holding his skeleton hand, while he shriveled in the hospital bed, watching *Family Feud* and wriggling the oxygen plugs from his nose to breathe in her second-hand smoke like it was heavenly ether. He'd look at me when I came in from school. I think I saw regret in his pain-bleary eyes. I saw remorse and maybe even an unspoken apology. But I ignored that shit like a beggar on the street. Fuck that. You don't get to beg for that. Not just because you're dying. Death ain't the almighty slate cleaner. It's just a fucking punctuation mark to the life you've lived. A good life is finalized by a simple period that is death. The rest, they labor in question, hanging like a thief from a gallows to be buried beneath a question mark. Or a comma.

Buddy... he didn't deserve nothing at all. He was a fucking scrap. A fragment.

For weeks after he died, mama was sad, though she *always* was. The silence in that mobile home had fists and punched almost as hard as she did, drunk. Didn't leave any bruises though. I remember just being mad that I never had the guts to take care of Buddy myself. I knew that was why Mimma had taught me the things she had, but I just didn't move to do nothin' about it. I sat in that trailer and watched mama crying every night. His air tank tubing clutched in her bony fist like precious pearls, while she wailed like a banshee. My stomach rolled at the silliness of it all. The brazen face slap of it all was that a man that messed with her little girl, under her nose in her own house, and she was carrying on like her Prince Charming had been killed trying to slay a dragon. I never really liked mama, but that feeling slid into full blown hate in those weeks.

It was a week before the end of September when I made the doll. I started with a tangle of hair from her brush and a stinking tampon fished from the bathroom trash. Her bleeding days were near an end, but the cork was slightly stained, and I figured the bond was set to be tight.

Can't judge a seed. Don't know no better than to grow or not. That's what Mimma always said.

Then I found one of her old nighties, a stupid fake silk thing that was wadded up between the bed and the wall. Probably thought lost after a feral night with Buddy who knew how long ago. I cut a ragged square from it and folded it over the stuffing. I wrapped the tampon with the hair, then a piece of tissue so it wouldn't soak through. I was committed but didn't want my fingers stinking like that. I was going for broke and fished out a handful of used dental floss from her bedside trash can. It was hard threading a needle with it but once I got it through...

I did it just like Mimma taught me. 'Cept I made it drag on some time longer, I figured I was owed.

The night I finished it, I dribbled a little pancake syrup over it and laid it under the porch. I wasn't in bed for more than half an hour before her shrieks filled the aluminum canister we lived in. I ran back, all concerned and fretting. When I saw the state of her sitting on her bed, it took all my resolve to not burst out laughing. The woman was naked, she almost always was when home. Her thin body was covered in bright red welts, long ribbons of weeping abrasions. Her sad tits. Mimma said once that Ma had tits like two fried eggs on a nail. They were weeping a cloudy discharge that trickled down over her ribs. I made a show of going to the bathroom and getting some itch cream and smearing it on her, tucking her into the sheets and then bringing her some itch pills. They were in fact some old Tic Tacs I found in the bottom of one of her old purses. She settled and I allowed my giggles to be free as soon as I closed the door. I grabbed a flashlight and snuck outside to retrieve the feejee. It was alive with ants and pinch bugs, so I rolled it in the grass until they were all off and took it inside. I wiped it as clean as I could with a wet paper towel and stowed it in the bottom drawer of my dresser. She'd had enough for today.

The next morning, I got up and got ready to head off to school. I grabbed the feejee from the drawer and took it with me into the hall. I listened close to Ma's bedroom door for sounds of movement, but all I heard was her snoring. I took the doll into the kitchen and unclipped the clothespins that made the little arms and legs. I put them in my backpack and stuck the rest of the doll under the pillows on my bed. I stood by the door, drinking the last of my orange juice before I hollered back to tell her I was leaving. It was after the fourth holler that I heard her voice muttering groggily.

"I can't feel my arms or legs. I can't move! Lyla? Lyla! Help your mama!"

I smiled and slipped out the door, slowly closing it and listening to the muffled sound as she continued yelling.

When I got home, the first thing that greeted me upon entering was the sour smell of piss. Under any other circumstances I'd have gagged, but I actually found myself smiling. I dropped my bag on the couch and went to my room to change. Mama must have heard me because she started yelling again, her voice was burlap rough and weak. Once I was in comfy clothes, I poked my head into her bedroom.

"Mama! What happened?"

I made a big show of rushing to her bedside. Of pulling back the sheet that was stained pale yellow and stinking. I made a concerned face when I saw the welts beginning to rise on her thighs and legs from where the urine had dried on her skin.

"I can't move. Feels like my arms and legs are gone. Can't feel 'em at all," she whimpered, and fat tears fled her eyes. I brought my hand to my mouth and feigned shock as I hid my smirk.

"Let me go get you some water and then we'll clean you up."

I walked slowly into the hall and ducked into my room to retrieve the feejee from my bed. I took it with me into the living room where I got the clothespins and clipped them back in place. I laid the doll on the couch and got the water for Mama before I went back to her room.

"That's wild. All of the sudden I got feeling back in my arms and legs, like some kinda magic trick." Her relief was thick on her face as she took the glass in her shaking hand and brought the water to her dry lips.

I chuckled and smiled at her. "That'd be some trick." I said.

She lasted almost an entire year before she was gone. Her absence was a thing I had rehearsed for practically my whole life, like some little girl playing rock star in the mirror or dreaming of being an actress. I pretended I was eulogizing mama and practiced doing it until I could go without laughing at the lies I'd tell. My sad smile should have gotten me a gold statue.

I left town the day after they fed her sorry husk to the worms. I packed my belongings into a single hardshell case and turned the oven on and up as high as the dial went. I opened it and tossed Mama's feejee into the square mouth before I kicked the door closed. By the time I had tied my boots and gave the place one last look around, it was dark outside. I grabbed the framed picture of Mimma that had hung by the door and made my escape. I stood on the dead lawn and watched while the trailer was coughing smoke into the night. Timber tall flames waving goodbye as I walked away from the long ugly first syllable of my life.

That was a few years back, before I landed here. Stuck in this toilet flush of a town like a crossway's turd. I got a trailer on the edge of town, rent's cheap, and I know what to do to make it cheaper. I got a job at the Buck Bonanza. It's a dump of a dollar store in the withering strip mall outside of town. It ain't a hard job. I run check-out and sometimes stock shelves. I got Buddy's old station wagon. Sometimes if I'm really tired, and I glance in the rearview, I think I see him plowin' mama in the back seat. There's a haunting you won't ever see on one of the TV shows.

I turned twenty-five last week. Weren't no fanfare. I got myself a little cake and ate it alone in my trailer. Time has a way, ya know, of taking things and making them sharp. Recollections in its grasp, rubbed along the unsmooth sides of it, become poison darts. Guilt is another son of a bitch. I know that them what I killed with the feejees deserved it. I know that my Mimma told me so. She taught me the trick and told me the rules. She told me how they work. That the dolls are mouths that eat the guilt, and since vile people are nothing but guilt and anger inside, it hollows them out to nothing. They eat themselves. I just wish Mimma had known a little more.

Like how a person who has known nothing but meanness and abuse their whole lives will feel guilty on account of it.

How even the act of roundabout revenge killing them what did it, would just set that guilt in cold hard stone. Like how if that person grew up and could never shake or reconcile that feeling of being unclean and unworthy that they might one day take it upon themselves to do bad things.

I started to notice the weight loss a few weeks back. I was always scrawny, but when I saw myself in the dirty bathroom mirror, my ribs were like one of those wooden xylophone things they had in music class. I figured something was wrong. I went to the clinic and got a look over. Nothing out of the ordinary to report, the cute student doctor said. He smiled when he said it. I smiled back and tried to play bashful. Would've worked better if I'd realized I had forgotten to button my shirt. I went home and looked at the feejees along the top of my dresser. I had saved them after I left home. They were tombstones. They were judgmental gods. They cried like babies in my dreams. I looked at them and the faded newspaper clippings pinned to each one. The black and white photos of the young men's faces. The words of love and remorse their family wrapped their deaths in to present a prettier loss.

I can't believe it had never occurred to me before. Or Mimma for that matter. You'd think she would have thought of it. I know why I'm losing weight. I see where my misstep was, and I know what I'll do with that knowledge.

I will make my own feejee with the napkin I spit Mark's cum into. It will have as much of me in it as him, as the others did. My spit, their seed. I'll sew it into a pair of my dirty panties, along with a handful of thumbtacks and rocks, and I will take time to make the end drag out. I want to feel the punishment. I want it to be like them South American priests that strip to the waist and flog themselves bloody in the shadow of the cross. I'll be bringing Mark along for the long and agonizing ride. I will crawl to his side when the end is near. When I can feel the teeth in my guts and the blood weep from my eyes. I will claw my way to his side and smile until he goes first.

My Mimma always said nobody is guiltless, and no one wants to die alone.

Like I did inside when I was ten years old.

SALTEN

Walking at night, I straddle two beaches, two seas.

Below my feet is one of wet sand and black singing water.

Above is another of sky and winking, swimming stars.

I keep walking, looking at my footprints from earlier.

Two and two and two until they stop.

The sand is torn, all prints erased.

Then there is one set.

Like the old poem.

"It was then that I carried you..."

—My skin was drying to sandpaper as I watched you put down your glass and rise from the bar.

Such beauty and lithe precision.

I waited for you to leave that place, and like a rumor, I followed.

You walked quickly, with a slight drunken stumble.

I moved as the night breeze.

"May I walk you home, you seem a bit unsteady," I said, my man mask on straight.

You smiled, a little flirty, "I guess so," you said, painted it with a laugh.

I steadied you by the arm, and we walked toward the beach.

The ocean whispered to me as a mother always does.

Such encouragement.

—We stopped by the rocks at the end of the path.

"I'm staying in that cottage there. With the light in the window."

I smiled and nodded and screamed beneath my mask, down in my coils and twists.

"Stay a bit longer. Let's talk and bathe in this night," I gasped and didn't remove my hand from her arm.

My fingers tightened.

She looked at me, and her smile tripped and fell into something a little like fear.

It was like a silent alarm to me.

I awakened with a jolt.

My eyes rolled over white.

A shark's eyes — like a doll's eyes...

"Wait until she sees me smile," I thought as I removed my mask.

The stars and sky have a hunger for screams, did you know that?

—I kneel beside my sea bride.

Bled dry and calcium white.

The stars reflecting in her eyes like Hollywood dreams.

Her mouth is open.

Her mouth is a shell.

With my hovering ear, I hear the swirling static sigh of waves and waves and waves.

I gasp and look out to the sea and up to the moon.

My brilliant teeth — points making a zig-zaggy grin, shine like diamonds.

They sing like an audience.

—I peel off my clothes before I peel off my skin.

The scales beneath are a thousand jewels stuck to my body.

—Her words were sand.

As were the ones before her.

Now dry and blowing in my eyes.

They had been damp and caked and clumped in my hair.

I was a drowned man dragged into the surf.

Fodder for crab and fish and gull.

I was a saltwater shadow slipping beneath a swimmer.

I was vast, and I was fathomless.

And with any luck, I would swim up again to bite her in two.

I was all those things.

Now they are all that I am.

And more.

Swirling in tide pools and in that dead girl's eyes.

NIGHT GAMES

They make no sound as they slink through the park. Shadows snaking around buildings and over or under fences. Phantoms in Keds and sweatshirts. They circle the stage area by the outhouses and pause. The old man sleeps here, beneath the arbor by the side park entrance. His drunken snoring sounds like chainsaw buzz. The stars glitter in the sky, and the long shadows surround him. He stirs once and settles back into his slumber. There is a small bubble nesting in the corner of his scabrous mouth. It grows and grows and then shrinks with his sour breaths.

Four small children, wearing plastic animal masks, stand in a semi-circle at his feet. The animal masks look ghastly in the moonlight: Piggy, Bunny, Kitty Kat, and Ducky.

Piggy looks down, and his breath condenses on the inside of his mask, nearly suffocating him with the stench of Cheerios and root beer. He sticks out his tongue and licks the moisture.

Ducky pours the gasoline while Kitty Kat lights the match. A hellish hiss and a sulfuric whiff of Hell, and it dances from her tiny fingertips. A fiery headed fairy diving toward damnation.

Bunny scampers back against the wall, the other three are her echoes. The old man manages one ragged scream before the flames melt his voice box. His coarse and wild beard blooms into a smoldering aura of fire and sizzling flesh. His rheumy eyes pop and sizzle and run like eggs. The flames dance in a combat orange reflection on the sheen of the masks the children wear. The stinking smoke climbs the night sky like a spectral ladder.

In less than an hour, the flames have died, and the man is still. His ragged clothing has melded with his flesh. He glistened wetly in the moonlight. Looking very much like a hog at one of the pig roasts they have in the park every summer. Bunny hops forward and hunches herself. The hem of her pink dress touches his thigh and absorbs sickly pink moisture from the body. She reaches out and grasps his left hand. Dexterous digits are now charcoal and bone, she snaps off a pinky and a thumb. She stands and scurries back to the wall. "Go," she chirps.

Ducky and Kitty Kat hold hands as they saunter to the smoking corpse. Kitty pulls his tongue from the skull, it stretches cartoonishly and finally snaps free. She stuffs it into her sweatshirt pocket and points to Ducky. The boy kneels and takes a bite of the dead man's ear. It crunches like his grandma's fried chicken. He chews and swallows and takes another bite.

When they return to the wall, Piggy takes his turn. He undoes his trousers as he approaches. The dead man hisses and steams as the piss hits the ruins of his face.

The church is hot and the sermon long. Darren and Jeff sit near the back. Jeff dozing lightly, as Darren contemplates the spiritual ramifications of cutting a fart in the house of God. He looks at his grandmother, and she shoots him a stern look that makes him rethink his urge. His stomach growls, and she shakes her head. The reverend goes on and on and on. Marcy sits beside her father, she fingers the hem of her dress, she is impressed she has gotten the stain out.

She looks up to the front row and sees Becky sitting next to her mother. She is thinking about her ballerina music box and the dead man's fingers that now live inside it. Her raven hair glistens and flutters in the breeze of the ceiling fans. While the preacher thinks about their souls and salvation. Their parents think about working and bills and survival. The children think about next Friday night, and what the game might be. Becky had suggested they switch masks this week. Darren likes this idea. Darren agrees with anything the girls say. Marcy was worried she'd get the Piggy mask. She grimaces at the recollection of Jeff licking the inside of his mask, disgusted. Boys were gross.

They all stand, and the organist introduces the hymn.

THE CLAIM

"*Every man is a book*," his mama used to say.

"*Don't be doin' nothin' you don't want on the pages, for sure as I'm standin' here, one day God's gonna read them pages and judge you by 'em.*"

That old gal would surely be spinning in her grave were she to lay eyes on the thumb-worn, tear-stained tome her boy had become. Sage words obliterated by the smudges of coal-black deeds.

Dandridge tried to ignore those thoughts, the memories that bore them, and tethered his horse to the wooden post in front of the saloon. He studied that post for a long moment. Its surface was scored with numerous wounds and scars. Stabbings and gunshots. Teeth marks from bored animals waiting for their owners to stagger out and ache their backs. It had witnessed victors and victims with stalwart and sun-faded indifference. He felt a kinship to this post. The whole damn town was like that post. Shit, the entire world. Just a gawking thing.

After a few more furtive glances over his shoulder, Dandridge patted the horse on the flank and went into the establishment. He could still feel the eyes of the folks in the street on his back like sticky tar. He usually swatted it all away and pretended like he had every right to be where he was, doing what he was doing. But the travel was wearing on him, and his nerves were gizzards hopping in a skillet. He smoothed down his focus as the swinging doors clacked behind him.

"What'll it be?" the barkeep asked, barely allowing Dandridge the time to make it to the bar, and without looking up from his wiping hand. Dandridge watched him in the cracked mirror on the wall. The sweat soaking the back of the man's shirt reminded him of a burial shroud, stained by the shape of what was once a living thing. The thought made him smirk.

"Whiskey, please."

"You new in town? Just passing through?" The bar man made eye contact while he poured, and that fact had Dandridge's insides dancing.

"Probably both."

"Sounds right. Not a place folks like to root down in and stick with." He replaced the bottle to the shelf and surveyed the half dozen or so drovers and derelicts that littered the establishment. "No one of any worth, anyway. Holler if you need a refill."

As quickly as he was there, the man vanished like a phantom, and Dandridge was alone with his glass and his always barking thoughts.

"HOWDY."

Dandridge closed his eyes as the scald of the last of the whiskey slid down his throat. He pursed his lips and sat the glass back on the bar.

"I says howdy to you." The voice was sopping with spit and reedy.

Dandridge gave the speaker the side eye and nodded.

"Howdy back." His lack of inflection would have hinted to any person with convention he didn't want to be bothered.

"Yer new?"

"Not really. I'm worn out as they come," Dandridge sighed and decided a little feigned social grace was in order, so he swiveled and held out a hand to the squirrely fella.

"My name's Dandridge, Lucas Dandridge."

The little man nodded enthusiastically, as though his head were threaded on some sort of wire. His eyes bulged slightly, and his forehead peeled from waning sunburn. He pulled the stinking hat on his head forward and took Dandridge's hand in both of his.

"Ren. You can call me Ren." He tittered a little and looked around the room. "Most of these folks don't call me at all. They's doctors and bankers and honest to God farmers, and so they think they're better. Maybe they are. Maybe they are." He continued to shake his head and giggle softly.

"What do you do then, Mr. Ren?" Dandridge felt his smile growing tight as church clothes.

"Ha! No need for the Mister. Just simple Ren'll do. Ain't been a Mister in my family since Pa kicked it."

"Okay. What is it you do, Ren?"

"That's much better. Much, much better. Well, Lucas, I have done and do many things. I have been everywhere and back again. I was young, and I am now not-so-young. I have seen things, and I have done my best to unsee things. But I assume what you mean is what do I do for my wage...currently, I help work a claim."

"Like gold digging?" Dandridge felt a surge of saliva in his mouth. Any mention of wealth had that effect on him. Greed had always been his favorite color.

"Jus' like that. I work with an old coot named Randall. He's a bit of a miserable sumbitch, but he feeds me and throws me some money when I need it. An' all I do is help him with whatever he needs me to. Diggin', haulin' out the dirt. Fetchin' supplies. Guardin'. Whatever."

"And he's doin' alright? He's found treasure?"

"Oh yeah, he's got a helluva claim goin' out there."

"Sounds like a good gig. Hard work is good for the soul, so's they say." Dandridge rapped his knuckles on the bar, and the barkeep appeared as if by an act of conjuring. He refilled the empty glass and turned to walk away. "Hold up, you want a drink, Ren?"

The smaller man giggled, and his eyes darted to the door and back. "Naw. I'm good. I never touch the stuff. It gets my nerves ta jumpin'. They jump enough as it is."

"Suit yourself." Dandridge drained his glass quickly and put his money on the table. He stood and turned towards his new acquaintance.

"You know how much the rooming house down the street runs? I'm getting low, but I don't have it in me to ride no more tonight."

"The hotel is two dollars a night. Real nice breakfast. And Miss Faber is mighty fine to behold. Mighty fine."

"All I got is two bucks, guess I could spend it on worse things."

"Surely, you could. For sure."

Dandridge squinted as he watched the twitchy man look around like he expected a posse to materialize and drag him away any second. He was like a mouse on a griddle, practically hopping in his skin.

"Think I'll go there then. Get a good night's sleep and see what I can get into tomorrow...find a job to get a few dollars together so's I can be on my way."

Ren followed him out and into the street, lingering awkwardly like a lonely child. Dandridge stood by his horse and untied it. He looked at the smaller man and nodded.

"Well, it was nice meeting you. Maybe I'll see you again before I pull up and move on."

Dandridge started down the street. Ren began to follow, almost timidly.

"Goodnight," Dandridge hollered over his shoulder and stopped. He heard the other man's footsteps cease as well. A loud sigh escaped Dandridge's lips, and he slowly turned to face his shadow.

"Look, I'm a nice man...really. I'm patient and friendly..."

Exceptin' you ain't always a nice man, Lucas Dandridge. You're a thief and a confidence man. You are a worm and a leech. You are blight with a handsome face who wraps himself in honest labor enough to look sharp and get the smell right. You can fool some of the people some of the time, but you can never fool yourself. The shit will always be on your boot, my friend. And that boot is always a kick away from your own snout. You're loathsome.

"But I'm beat. Dog tired. I just wanna go and get into a bed and sleep."

The little man nodded and turned to head back to wherever it was he came from. Dandridge started walking, giving a slight tug on the reins to guide his horse. It was hardly a minute later when he heard the small steps behind him again. "Hey. Um. Lucas. I just had me a thought."

DOES THIS LITTLE shit ever shut that mouth of his?

Dandridge sat on his horse and watched as the light bled from the sky. A dollop of yolk on a dead man's chin was what the sunset looked like. He snicked and pulled the rein a little, and the horse trotted a little faster, sidling up alongside Ren and his mule.

"I shoulda gotten a good night's sleep and met up with you in the morning. Though, still havin' my money feels kinda nice." Dandridge glanced over and saw the little man's lips moving like ants on scraps. He heard almost no evidence he was speaking, as the whispers were hardly competition for the breeze.

Ren noticed his new friend's stare and smiled wide and sheepish. "You okay, Ren?"

"What?" The smaller man was startled by the sudden voice in the not-really-quiet. "Yeah, I'm fine. I ain't so good at night, so I have to count and figure my directions. Desert gets bigger when it gets blacker."

"Makes sense. We could go back to town and wait for the sun."

"We ain't that far. I know where we are. Not far at all." Ren patted the mule's neck, and it walked a little faster. A little.

A few paces behind, Dandridge sat in his saddle and watched the mule's ass like a beacon. He chewed his lip and thought about sacks bulging with gold.

"Ren, you goddamn rat, where have you been?" The voice, full of raw edges and wound inflicting, was a cannon blast in the night. Dandridge was just ambling into the timid glow from the firelight when Ren got the first cuff upside his head.

"You know I like ya back by sundown. I got work to do down there, need you here to watch up top!"

The second slap wasn't as hard, but still sounded like someone dropping a cabbage. Ren rubbed at his reddening face and apologized through quivering lips.

Dandridge came into the light and jumped down from his horse in a fluid motion, not even bothering to tie the leather to anything.

"That'll be enough of that." Dandridge took a step towards Ren, and the old man stooped before him. His nostrils flared at the rancid stink rolling off the old coot in foul waves. Sweat, soured milk, and something else. He swallowed the thickness that rose in his throat.

"No need to be hitting anyone."

"I don't believe I know you, sir." Words spat from the toothless hole in a nest of wrinkles and whiskers. They were wrapped in reeking breath.

"You do not. Name's Lucas Dandridge. Drifter for hire." He held out a hand, and the old man looked at it like it was dipped in shit.

"Folks hire you to drift?"

"No. I'm a drifter…but I'm open to do whatever work pays."

"Oh, I get it." The old man spit into his hand and wiped the muddy brown from the palms onto pants that were just as dirty. "I'm Micah. Micah Randall. Sorry about that abhorrent spectacle you just witnessed. I lose my temper with that boy sometimes. He's what my ma used ta call 'spooky'."

Micah offered his hand, and Lucas took it. It felt stone-rough against his warm skin.

"You've come to help work the claim then?"

"Well, I suppose that's the plan. Ren just said you had a claim, and you were old and could use the extra help, a strong back as he put it."

"Ren tells the truth. Though sometimes sussin' it outta all the other babble that pours out that mouth is a near Biblical test of faith and patience in itself. He helps me some, but he lacks focus, I guess you could say. Down in the hole. I need help with digging and carrying out the dirt. Not much help if you are prone to disappearing to wander around and mumble to yourself."

"No, I'd wager not."

The old man picked up the pot from where it hung over the fire and poured a cup of steaming dark liquid. He held it out to the new arrival and then poured another for himself.

"Coffee, and then we get to work."

"I was hoping to get some sleep first, I've been riding for four days. Opted for this over a night at the hotel in town."

"I'll just show you the ropes. Explain what I need, and how you can help. Then you can sleep. I prefer to work at night mostly, much cooler. And at my age, comfort is the patibulum of my cross."

Dandridge had no idea what that word meant, but politely nodded, took the offered cup, and sipped his coffee, hiding the wince when the bitter earthy flavor hit his tongue.

— — —

The ladder was a rickety thing that bowed and creaked under his weight. Though the hole only went down about eight feet, Dandridge kept his eyes forward and didn't look down. He hopped off the bottom rung and looked up at the mouth of the pit. A few jutting rocks actually made it resemble one, beyond that a gullet full of stars.

"This way then." The old man moved fast for his posture and age. Hunched and purposeful in motion. Dandridge made to follow and had only the rope of shadow behind the other man to hold on to.

The tunnel was not long, perhaps twenty or thirty feet. Roughly gouged from the earth with slats and barn wood against the sides to offer support. Pale stones cropped up like occasional faces. A single lantern drooled feeble light from its hook. Dandridge marveled at the progress an old man like Micah had made, seemingly by himself.

"How long it take you to dig all this?"

"Oh, I don't know. Six months, maybe. Mighta been ten. I got no stock in time these days." He stooped and gripped the shovel and pick from where they leaned against the earthen wall.

"You strike yet?" Dandridge asked and tried his best to keep that feral edge from his voice, the one that sometimes showed itself when his mask slipped a little. The old man stood almost straight but didn't turn.

"A little. But more like a schoolyard kiss, a promise of what might wait beyond patience."

"How little?" The edge was evident that time, and Dandridge decided he didn't really care.

"I have a couple bags of dust and small nuggets, good for a thousand dollars maybe...I feel certain that deeper in is bigger and better."

Micah turned and held the handles of the tools out towards the other man.

"Pick your poison, young fella."

DANDRIDGE KEPT HIS eyes closed but could still tell the difference in the blackness he saw. There were lighter spots that shook where beyond closed lids the campfire danced. Darker shades of pitch where the night loomed over him. He was dog-tired, but the internal dialogue running in his brain was incessant. It muttered of gold and wealth. Of women and cards. Between the drone in his head, and the faded mumble of the voices from the claim, Dandridge surrendered to sleep.

"TIME TO GIT up."

Dandridge opened a sleepy eye and saw Ren's homely face above him. The sun was high above him, surrounding his head with a halo of light. The man had a hand held out. Dandridge ignored it as he sat up and rubbed his neck. He licked his palm and smoothed down errant hair and plopped his hat on for cover.

"I feel like I ain't slept but an hour or two."

"Try nearly ten. Micah worked until sunup, and then he bedded down and said you was to take over where'n he stopped."

Dandridge looked around the scrawny camp. Aside from the tangle of bedroll where he currently sat, there was no other sign of anyone down for rest. Ren read the befuddlement on the new man's face. "He's in the hole. It stays cool down there. That old man can't take the heat, but he could sleep through a dynamite blast...I'll tell you that."

Dandridge stood and stretched.

"I'll have some coffee and maybe a little to eat before I head down, that okay?"

"Certainly. I got coffee made, and there's a satchel by the rocks, full of cornbread and tack. It ain't much, but it keeps out here well enough."

"It's fine. I'm obliged."

Dandridge broke off a hunk of staling cornbread and washed it down with sour coffee. Ren paced back and forth, his hands fluttering like birds. He was a curious one.

"So, how much have you two pulled out so far? I mean, I ain't doubtin' ya, but from here this looks like a sorry operation. An old man and a…a unique feller like yourself digging for gold in the desert. A shovel and a pick and a broke down mule. Not much for food." He paused to drain his coffee and tossed the last chunk of cornbread into the eager fire. "Just seems all around poorly, I guess."

"Naw. No, we do good. Micah has bags of his gold. I helped. I'm a helper." Ren got more fidgety, and his pacing grew in urgency.

"Calm yourself, son. I'm just surmisin'. I wanted to figure whether my help was needed or even worth givin'."

"To give of one's self is always worthy." Ren replied, the look of abject pleasure when he said it was notable, like a child who had memorized his first Bible verse.

Dandridge nodded, bent to retrieve the shovel from where it lay near the entrance to the hole, and made his way down the ladder.

--- --- ---

HE WAS SURPRISED he'd even bothered with the pretense of helping at all, but Dandridge put in a solid few hours of digging and carrying crumbling earth to the ladder before stopping. He wiped the sweat from his brow and rested against the damp sides of the pit. It was quiet save for his heavy breathing and the light snores coming from the small chamber off from the short tunnel.

How does he sleep down here in this dank damp? Smells like the bottom of a gravedigger's boot.

Dandridge slowly crept along the wall and peered into the tiny room. A small lantern sat on the floor by the far wall and pissed faded light around it. The earthen walls absorbed the light and fed it back weaker. To the right side of the entrance was a tangle of blanket covering a prone form. The man slept with his toothless mouth open, and a buzz like an angry beehive rose from it. The line that dragged his gaze was the several bags along the wall at the old man's feet. Nearly eight of them, every one bulging and tied with twine. Dandridge smiled, and his skin danced at the prospect of stealing them and the gold they held. He picked up the shovel and licked his lips.

The old man's eyes popped open at the touch of metal against his throat. "What the…"

Dandridge bared his teeth and brought his boot down on the shovel blade. Dulled by rocks and dirt, it pushed down through sagging skin and bone. Micah's eyes bulged, and tears flowed freely down pale, stubbled cheeks.

With a weary sigh, Dandridge raised a foot and brought it down - once more – harder, and the blade broke skin and separated ver-tebrae. One more stomp, and the shovel edge kissed the dirt floor. The old man's eyes scowled at him as they lost their light, and as his breathing ceased, the chamber was silent save for Dandridge's own shallow breaths and the light burble of flowing blood.

Still easier than all that diggin'.

Dandridge sneered at the dead man and knelt to collect his new wealth.

DANDRIDGE HUNKERED BY the fire. Ren was nowhere in sight. Most likely wandering the nightscape, chattering with the coyotes or playing with scorpions. Dandridge grabbed the first of the five bags he'd brought up and emptied its contents onto the hard clay before him.

Rings. Easily two hundred rings. Some gold, some silver. Some dainty and others large gaudy things. Maybe another hundred necklaces. Over two dozen pocket watches. Countless earrings. Brass buckles and cufflinks. Brooches. There was a harmonica and a sterling silver baby's rattle.

Puzzled, the man picked another sack and untied it, poured its innards with the rest. Coins. Hundreds of silver pieces and gold circles. More rings and several pairs of eyeglasses with silver frames. Wads of paper money tied with twine.

Cold sweat began to trickle down Dandridge's back.

The moon was witness to a fool. A greedy fool. Killed again... an old man for bags full of loot he stole himself.

There were still three or four more bags down there. Maybe they really held the bragged-of gold. If not, he could take it all and ride well into a town...far enough away he could sell the stuff and move on. Another stain on the shitty britches of his conscience made no never mind at all. He sighed and went back down in the hole.

THE FIRST THING Dandridge did before he gathered up the remaining bags was toss the blanket of the dead coot's face. He didn't need the man's eyes watching him. Odd that one act of treachery nary ruffles a feather but one can be seemingly bashful of another. Dandridge turned to grab the last bag when he heard a noise from the other room. A sound that promised something large being dragged above ground. He cocked his head and listened harder. A giggle fluttered down like a bat.

Ren.

Shovel in hand, he left the last bag and made his way back into the main chamber. The silver fall of moonlight that had flowed through the hole above was gone. A splinter of panic worked its way into the meat of his being. Dandridge dropped the tool and ran to the foot of the ladder. He stared up at the opening, sealed off by what appeared to be an old door. The cobwebby threads of light that wormed through the edges danced on the brass of the knob. There came a rapping on the other side. The outer side.

"Knock, Knock."

Ren laughed like a small child. His voice withered to a whisper, and he talked to another or himself, though it was unintelligible. Dandridge went back for the lantern and the pickaxe.

THE HAND HOLDING the lantern was sweating, all of him was, but the left hand more so. It felt as though the hand might burst into flame at any second. Dandridge worked the flat side of the pick under the edge of the door and pushed with all his might. Not even a groan or falling clod of dirt for his effort.

He balanced the lantern on the rung and tried again with both hands. Nothing. This time, the lantern fell from its perch and hit the floor with a clunking crash. There was barely enough oil left to spark a decent fire, but fickle light briefly illuminated the bones that were piled in the back end of the room. Lots of them. Then, the darkness swooped in and ate the light before it really came to be.

He had just started climbing back down when he heard the sounds. Movement in the dark. It was a sliding sound, mixed with a slight squeaking.

Rats! Had better not be fucking rats!

He jumped the last few rungs and landed with a thud, amazingly keeping his balance. Dandridge knelt, pulled the hand-kerchief from his vest pocket, and swabbed the ground around the broken lamp. Tiny teeth of glass chewed on his fingers and the remains of the oil licked them stung. He wrapped the cloth around the handle of the pick and lit it with a match. He wished he hadn't as soon as the light barged in.

The old man stood *above* the floor, hovering inches over the packed dirt. His gnarled toenails had dragged small grooves in his approach from the other chamber. The front of his filthy nightshirt was black with blood. He held his almost severed head up onto his neck with hands tipped in long nails. The eyes that nested in it were cotton white and owlish.

But what made Lucas Dandridge start to lose his cruel mind, made the thief piss his pants, was the old man's mouth. A yawning cavern overflowing with teeth. Long thin points and thick triangles of bone fought for a chance at the air from the devilish hole in his face. The hands moved and allowed the head to nod, and that mouth rose into a smile.

"The claim…" was all Dandridge managed to utter before the moonlight poured down over him as Ren pulled away the door.

"Is all you ever were," Micah spoke, the voice a cistern whisper that came from ragged lips as well as the stump of his neck. "Always…"

Dandridge dropped the torch so he wouldn't see those teeth as they came for him. But fate wouldn't stand for that and allowed it to burn on the floor long enough for him to see good and well.

THE SWARTHY FELLOW walked into the saloon like he owned it. He only looked over his shoulder a few times. He was getting better. He was barely to the bar when the man tending it barked at him.

"What can I get you?"

"A beer." He looked around at the sorry lot in the place. Old card players and fat drovers. Harlots and sod busters. He felt the weight of his gun belt, and a warm smile blossomed.

"Howdy!"

The stranger sipped his mug and made no gesture of acknowledging who spoke.

"I says howdy to you, Mister."

A shadow fell over his beer hand, and the man looked into the beady eyes of what might have been the dirtiest sumbitch he'd ever seen…or smelled. The dirty little man opened his mouth and leaned forward.

"Mah name's Ren. You here lookin' fer work?"

IN THE MORNING

Norman sat at the table, eating his cereal. He faced the far wall of the room. A blazing white blank. Forty square feet of drywall and plaster. The tongues were wagging. They jutted from the wall every four inches, like glistening skinned thumbs. Norman took spoonfuls of soggy wheat and flung them against the wall. The tongues strained to catch the droplets of food. Norman took a bite for himself and flung some more. When he was finished, he stood and walked towards the wall, unbuckling his pants as he did so.

DOODLEBUG

1.

"That girl over there pouting by the shed again?" Mrs. Amber spoke in her succinct manner, almost biting words in half. Not as haughty as her voice would misdirect you to think. Just the way she came across.

"Probably," her mother had replied, pausing to swallow smoke and spew it into the drab air around them. "If misery were water, and woe was liquid dinosaur, our little Marta'd be the best dowser around," her mother had said, so matter-of-factly, that it was akin to a mild sweep of the hand to shoo a gnat. Marta kept her back to the women, their words bouncing off of her slightly stooped spine like falling acorns.

2.

THAT RECOLLECTION ECHOES in Marta's mind, like the honking of autumn geese making their escape before that first snow. She stares at the house as it bleeds orange fists of flame, disgorges thick coils of smoke into the early morning sky. She stays behind the rest of the crowd, behind the yellow tape that flutters in the air. Air that's filled with the wrestling smells of scalded metal and that underlying tang of cooked meat — all of them congregating and ushering her into a sermon of destruction and death. She stays back behind the rest, craning her neck to watch the firemen carrying out the three stretchers. Stretchers bearing cargo less than half their length.

The smells of water and ash, of rendered wood.

She notes the plastic playhouse in the side yard near the burning structure, warping from the heat. The men's faces are bright red and slicked with sweat or tears, not much difference, is there? Salt water is salt water. Marta looks at her feet. Her white sneakers speckled with ashen mud. She hears one of the firemen bellow for more water, and she bites her lip. She bites hard enough to feel the edge of a tooth break skin, taunt blood, and swallow it. Her skin is dancing. She looks at what is left of the house — a charred skull devoid of flesh — and beholds it as the castle of her dreams. A smile threatens to bubble up, but she bites her lip even harder, and that stops it. There is a tremendous sound as the back portion of the roof caves in, she imagines it being under the weight of the fist of God. She deeply inhales another lungful of the smells and turns to walk away.

She keeps walking, and in her mind, she walks backwards over years as cracked as the sidewalk.

3.

"WHERE'S THAT GIRL now?" Pa's voice was tilted and stumbling over his tongue. He was drunk again. She heard him stomping through the trailer. Frankenstein foot thumps on plywood covered with thin carpet remnants.

"She's out burning the trash," her mother answered.

"What, is she gonna crawl in that barrel herself?" the man sneered and laughed that bloody kicked thing he called a laugh. Then there was no sound from inside the home. A place where silence had a tendency to grow fists and hit hard, and where quiet almost always gave birth to tears and bruises.

Marta stood out in the far corner of the yard, beside the leaning garage, and peered into the depths of the burn barrel. The flames down there devoured everything she tossed in, they were as starved dogs in a pit - snapping and chewing up whatever was thrown to them. The newspapers and old catalogs. The cardboard trays the beer came in. The flames ate it all and were never full. She felt the warmth on her face as she watched the fire whirl and dance. She held her hands just above the rim of the barrel, the heat from the metal lightly pushing against her palms like a kitten's paws. She closed her eyes and listened to the crackle and hiss of it. It whispered to her a poem of devotion and devastation. Her heart beat faster, and sweat coated her pale skin. She stood there and prayed with the burning, and in her self-imposed darkness she saw shadows scuttle and scurry behind shrouds of smoke and pillars of angry orange. They rose high into the sky before a castle of flame. Windows bowed and melted, and from behind them faces screamed. She smelled hot metal and charred paper, and with her eyes still closed and her mind still dreaming, she smiled. The saliva that coated her teeth dried in the heat that *caressed her face. She had witnessed Heaven, and it was beautifully burning.*

Inside the trailer, there was a loud crack, and something made of glass broke, whimpering followed.

4.

MARTA AWOKE FROM dreams filled with smoke and bright orange kisses. Faces of people she once loved or never loved all reduced to cinderous visages that crumbled and blew away. She rubbed an arm across her drooling mouth and smelled the thick sweat that sheened her. It was like she was slick and fresh from the womb. She nearly smiled. She looked at the clock on the box that served as a nightstand. The zeroes blinked and blinked. She sighed through her teeth and sat up, allowing the stinking sheet to slide from her chest. She looked down at her pallid breasts and the freckles that lived there. She felt the corners of her mouth droop, a divining rod that's found water. She stood and stomped into the bathroom. Sitting on the toilet, she lit six matches as she stared at herself in the mirror over the sink. She gazed at her plain face through the flame of each match and let them burn until they hissed out against calloused fingertips. She ate every one, and to every one she assigned a name. More than one was called Papa. She looked at herself and turned away, she was always prettier through heat waves. She began brushing her teeth and did not stop until the foam she spat was berry red.

5.

IN PICTURES SHE is char and bone. Black crackle and tooth. A handful of diamonds scattered on fresh tar. Of all the fires she's started...the ones behind her eyes burn with the most ferocity.

Memories are inexhaustible fuel. She watches as the corner of the picture starts to curl as the wisps of black smoke start their serpentine crawling in the air. She looks at the girl in the photograph. The girl looked just like her, only younger and smaller and rounder of face. The gingham shirt. The stringy hair. Marta frowned and waited for the girl to burn. She'd spent all these years waiting for that girl to burn. She held it until her fingertips grew hot, and then she let it drop from them. It fluttered like a wounded dove until it landed on the pile of papers on the porch. Marta waited for the consummation of flame and newsprint. The ferocious copulation that would explode and climax with full-blown fire and fury. Marta stepped back around the truck that was parked there and peered around the rusted bumper. She watched the window of the house. The curtains did not flutter. The *Oxygen In Use* sign in the window. She watched as the flames began to devour the porch and lick the door. She imagined she heard a voice from inside. A raspy plea for help. In her head it was her mother, and so she paid it little mind. She watched as the trailer twisted in on itself like a diseased spine, bleeding smoke into the overcast sky. Marta started back home and kept her head down as the fire trucks sped by.

6.

"WHAT DO YOU want out of life?" the man with the notepad asked teenage Marta. She sat on the couch and fiddled with the small hole in the leg of her jeans. Feeding it her fingers so it could grow.

He stared at her patiently. His eyes were warm, and he had a sad smile on his face. "Marta?" he paused and leaned forward, elbows on his knees. "What would you like more than anything in the world?"

"To burn," she muttered and never took her focus off of the hole that was enlarging with the help of her probing fingers.

"That's what got you here. You burned down a school building and a shed."

"Not to burn as verb. To burn as destiny," she looked at the man, and he did not look away.

"Why is that?" he asked.

"I've been doing it since the day I was born. I always burn inside."

The man closed his notepad and stood up from his chair. He went to the desk and gave her a fraudulent smile as he picked up the phone and pushed some buttons. Marta worked at making the hole even bigger, while in the background the man spoke in the hushed tone of spies.

7.

MARTA SITS AT her desk and lets the phone ring. She has her earpiece plugged into the jack, so the droning ring is unheard by the others in the office. She stares at the computer screen and allows the electronic trilling to invade her head. She flares her nostrils and thinks she smells smoke. A quick glance as the snobby girl from the adjacent cube walks by, fresh from a cigarette break. Marta closes her eyes and inhales deeply. She recalls wishing she were the ash of a cigarette, to be flicked to the wind and ride it to everywhere. She remembers being envious of the Pompeiians. She sniffs again and fantasizes she is the smoke squirming through the woman's lung tissue. Exchanging breath for cancer like bleak currency. Marta feels her mouth flood with saliva. She swallows it and it tastes of sulfur. The phone has stopped ringing, but her ears have not.

8.

SHE WAS RELEASED from the juvenile center a few days before her eighteenth birthday. She was already approaching eighty in her mind. Wrinkles in time and short-circuits of thought had been a constant for years. She was old when she slid from that rancid womb, she thought as she ascended the small porch and opened the door. The sticking stink of too many cigarettes in too small a space greeted her like an anxious dog. She stepped over the shoes and boots strewn inside the doorway and into the living room. She sat on the sunken thing that was once a couch and looked at the ancient coffee table before it. Scoured with cigarette burns and marked with so many cup rings it looked like the underside of a tentacle. She saw a newspaper and picked it up.

She saw the pipe and the empty baggies underneath it, wishing they'd scurry from sight like pill bugs. She looked around the room. The house she'd lived her entire life in - a long aluminum box on flat tires. Filled with sweat and anger and more misery than the Old Testament. She held her breath and heard the ragged snoring from the back bedroom. She looked at the clock on the wall and saw that it marked the time as 2:35, just as it had for the last decade or so.

Marta rolled the newsprint in her hands and walked back the length of the trailer's hall. The worn carpet whispering secrets to the bottoms of her shoes. She peeked into the bedroom and saw the piles of stinking laundry. Saw the sheet covered forms on the sagging bed. Saw the hairy forearm of her father hanging over the side. That awful jailhouse tattoo of a tiger looking more like an ink sketch on a napkin that got wet. Marta bit her lip and pulled the door closed. She tied the pantyhose around the knob and stretched them to the bathroom door where she did the same. Pulling it as tight as possible. She reached into her jacket pocket and pulled out the Bic. She bought it at the Qwik Mart down the street once she was out of sight of the state bus that dropped her off. It was blue and had a fish painted on it, leaping gape-mouthed at a dragonfly. She flicked the wheel, and the flame appeared. She touched it to the newspaper in her other hand and held it a second or two until they were well acquainted. She laid it down on the carpeting and put a few pieces of laundry nearby for it to eat. She went back to the front of the trailer.

9.

AS THE SUN *sank and the trailer burned. Long after the muted screaming stopped, Marta still stood at the edge of the field and watched. This was the only time she could recall being appreciative of her father's insistence at living out in the sticks. She watched the ashes dance in the glow. They were memories. That big one dancing over by the fallen-down shed might have been the time he broke her collarbone. The small one that landed on her lapel was the time her mother told her to just be quiet and things will be easier. "Silence is golden for a reason, pumpkin," she had slurred before she dropped the bottle in her claw.*

Marta closed her eyes and stepped forward with her mouth opened as wide as she could.

10.

THE BREEZE THAT slithered through the screen was humid and thick. It undulated rather than blew across the room. Marta lay on top of her bedding. Bathed in silver and shadow. Her pale skin was downright alabaster in the darkness. She stared at the ceiling and watched the shadows flex and whisper there. She interpreted their secrets and filed their promises. She remembered the first moment she realized she was a myth. A walking, talking anecdote that was easily ignored and sharply forgotten at will. She was always the stain on the carpet in the corner of the room. The stain on her parents in the corner of their lives. She was just always. She sniffed back the tears that were running down her face and smiled a little lopsided thing. On the dawdling air was the scent of charcoal and flame. That flammable lullaby sang her to sleep.

11.

THE DAY AFTER she turned twenty-four: The man sits in the chair. He hardly ever holds the notepad anymore. The pen stays in the stupid pocket of his stupid pressed shirt. He tents his fingers and touches the tip of his nose and spits out his questions like darts.

"How are we doing with the memories?" The question is drab beige paint on drywall.

"I eat them and never seem full," she replies.

"They aren't very filling, are they?" A small chuckle goes ignored.

"I'll spell it out for you. You take a memory. Pull it out slow. Dip it in that cloudy cup of nostalgia and lay it on the table before you. See if that helps. Usually doesn't for long. They aren't always pretty. Often, they twist and squirm like that fat ol' worm when you lift the rock it lives under. Happier to be in the dark and wriggling in the mud and pitch black. Happier isn't always in the vocabulary though. Sometimes happiness is just nine letters someone scrawled on the shithouse wall when they were out of paper."

The man reaches out for his tablet, lets his forefinger touch the corner but does not pick it up.

"What are we after here, exactly?" The eyebrow above his left eye is the top point of a triangle.

"I'm not sure. The court made me come here, remember?"

"I do. But I feel as though we're not mining any new ore."

"Sorry to be boring you."

"You know that isn't what I meant."

"Do I?"

"You do."

"Ask another of your questions."

"When your parents died...after all of the abuse you suffered at their hands, did that feel freeing? It's completely normal to answer yes."

"It felt earned." Marta paused and felt out the words eager to leap from her tongue for betrayal. "My papa was a beast and my ma his shadow.

When I got the call they'd been killed, I was sad, but it was more a reflex than an actual feeling. The indifference felt like a new pair of shoes, a size too small."

The man slowly nodded and touched the pen in his pocket but did not remove it. "Do you miss them?"

"Only as a person who's lost a limb might miss it after the stump has healed. It's gone but they still feel it. My parents were phantom limbs well before they were dead."

He looked at the clock. "2:35. Session is over. You know you never answered me when I asked why you wanted your hour to end at 2:35 every time."

"Because that's when the time ends. It's been like that for years." Marta slipped out the door with no further banter. The man put his pad and pen in his desk and loosened his tie. He could smell the sweat that soaked his undershirt.

12.

SHE SAT ON the back steps of her building, the cigarette nestled between her fingers emitting curls of smoke. She put it to her lips and brought them into her lungs. She felt them swirl and swim like tadpoles. She held the cigarette upright and touched the glowing tip to the string dangling from the cuff of her sleeve. She waited for the fabric to darken and flare a little. The flame sniffing for purchase before growing. She held her arm still and waited for it to blossom. Small petals of fire dancing on denim. She saw the police car approach from the opposite side of the intersection, so she blew out the infant flame like a birthday cake candle. She would add it to her growing list of almosts. She often felt like that's all she was.

13.

"YOU'RE VERY PRETTY." The boy with the hair in his eyes said, his eyes darting like little fish when she tried to catch them.

"Thank you," she heard herself reply. Had she ever said those words before? They sounded nonsensical.

"I see you sitting out here all the time. I live in the apartment above you." So awkward, he was. She smiled and nodded. She looked over the edge of the steps at the collection of debris and trash deposited there by a myriad of storms. Paper cups and plastic wrappers and a population of cigarette butts. She flared her nostrils and smelled their wet, ashen reek. She felt him still there, still looking at her, but he'd turn his face away slightly when she caught him looking at her. "I hear you up there sometimes, you try and walk softly." She raised the corners of her mouth a bit.

He smiled and nodded. "I try to." She just looked at him, and he at her. The night stretched like shadow taffy. The silence was pregnant but would need a cesarean section. Taking the hint, the boy nodded again and held out his slender hand.

"My name is Roy. I guess I'll catch you around."

"I'm Marta," she whispered, it sounded like blasphemy. She took his hand in her much smaller one. She felt the scar that lived on the back of his, raised and smooth, a burn. She smiled and looked him in the eye. "I'm pleased to meet you." He freed his hand and went up the steps and in through the door. If he had done it any faster, he would have been running. Marta stood and touched her face with the hand that had grasped his. She felt her freckled skin. It was flushed and warm. She heard sirens in the distance and the sounds of a television wafting above her. She went inside and into her apartment. And dreamed of burning in the arms of a boy named Roy.

14.

"YOU KNOW THIS is our last session?"

"I don't need you anymore. I'm normal." Her smile is an uneasy thing.

"No one is saying that, I don't believe a normal person exists." He smiles as well, his fits better.

"What are you going to do?"

"Keep on keepin' on as they say. I have dreams like everyone else. I'll try and live them."

"That's a good strategy to start with. Marta, you have my number, I'm always around if you need me."

"I know."

"Let's chat a bit before we say our fond farewells...what's this week dealt you?"

"I smell ashes and mud, and it makes me homesick."

The man nods and does the little circular thing with his hand that tells her she's to continue.

"I met a boy, and he was kind to me. Smiled at me. Said I was pretty."

"That's great."

"He lives above me in my building."

The man nods again and taps his upper lip with his index finger. "Do you think anything will come of it?"

She shrugs, and her shirt rides up from her midriff. He sees her navel and the scar that neighbors it. He looks away quickly. He stands and leans over her, both hands on her shoulders. "I've greatly enjoyed the time we've had all these years, what is it? Four? I've seen you make a lot of peace within yourself. I think you're ready for the world, and with any luck, it will be ready for you." He steps back, and she rises like heat and smoke and floats right out the door.

15.

ROY HUNCHES OVER his desk and draws the monster. It towers protectively over the frail girl with the freckles and the wayfaring smile. Her eyes are sad. He mutters to himself as he renders her. He looks at the clock and sees it is after two in the morning. There is a knock at his door, timid and small.

"Who is it?" he calls, and it sounds weak and uneasy.

"Marta," she replies, and he opens it and invites her in with a sweep of his arm. The hallway is hazy.

He wrinkles his nose, "There a fire somewhere?"

"There always is."

"I mean, did you walk by one? I smell smoke, and it's strong."

"I don't know."

"I need to finish this artwork, you can watch and talk to me while I work on it if you want."

She nods, and he sits and picks up the pen. She watches the shine of his scarred hand fence with the light of his lamp. She lets it dance in her eyes and smiles. He looks at her, and his hand stops moving. She lays her hand on top of his, and he does not pull away.

"How?" she asks.

"Fire."

"When?"

"Forever."

"That's the way."

Outside, the sound of sirens grows louder, closer. The flashing red lights paint the walls and windows in strobing rubies.

"What's going on?" Roy asks, but he does not rise or take his hand from under hers, his eyes from hers.

"We are." she whispers. Smoke curls a finger under the door and then another.

At 2:35, they begin to smolder.

THEM IRON EYES
CODY BLUES

Temple stabbed his walking stick into the scorched earth. It wept and gave purchase to the staff.

Groaning, he knelt by the river. It used to flow free and wild. A liquid snake that seethed and hissed. Now, its fetid waters were congealed with poisons and monsters. The shoreline glistened with beads of mercury that caused the dead fish and bottles that bobbed there to shimmer in the dull sunlight. Like a scab forming at the edges of a wound. Once in a while, a slick tentacle or pincer claw would break the syrupy surface to pick at the floating dead. Swollen and rolling on the slow current like maggoted buoys. Bobbing near the water's edge, close to where he hunkered, was a large white lily.

He reached for the lily cluster and smiled. His eyes watered as he tried to capture the most beautiful thing he had seen since society shit the bed. The tears may have been from the fumes as well. They rolled from the water's surface in waves that were practically visible. His numb fingers grazed the viscous current and grabbed the petals. The slimy bottom felt like a phlegm-coated sponge.

A baby's soft spot. He lifted it to his watering eyes and lowered the crusty surgical mask. It wasn't a lily. It was a rotting head of cabbage. Its yellowed surface teeming with insects, wriggling and struggling to stay above the water level. He dipped it into the glowing swirls of water and shook the droplets and the agitated vermin free. They splattered the caked mud of the beach like blood spray. He pulled the mask away again and took a bite of the rotten vegetable. Thick ooze squirted from the sides as his brittle teeth tore into the addled meat of the vegetable. He belched and gagged but willed it down. His stomach was so empty, it literally sounded like someone dropped a rock into a dried up well. He held his jaw firm, allowing the vomit and acid to rise, to tickle the back of his teeth and then recede. Pink snot began to trickle from his nose. He closed swollen eyes and smiled. In his mind, the cabbage was a fresh apple from his grandfather's orchard. He was basking in the warm sunlight as the sweet juice glazed his chin. Addy coughed, and that gunshot sound jarred Temple back to their festering reality.

Addy stood to the side. The smoky breeze fondled his greasy hair. He sighed as he watched Temple eat the cabbage. "No ships, no sealing wax," Addy spoke. His voice, a skull splitting under rock. A fly landed on his ear and crawled inside. Addy never flinched. The fly never returned.

"So hungry, I'd have eaten kings," Temple countered and spat at his feet. The blood made it look like a ruby. He handed the remaining half of the cabbage to his friend. "I fear we might be the only two folks left who know about *Alice In Wonderland*." He swept an arm in a melodramatic gesture to the landscape. "The looking glass we've gone through is cracked and melted."

"I'd be sad that you're correct as usual, had I enough gumption to give a shit anymore," Addy grumbled, a post-apocalyptic

Eeyore. Something in the river pulled a large rat from the edge of the water, and its legs kicked as it was pulled under the sludge. Temple rose to his staggering full height and took up his blackened walking stick. The muck of the riverbank gasped.

Addy raised his - a javelin he had taken from the gymnasium so long ago. It had a white flag on it. A flag was made from one of his old dress shirts from when he was a teacher, and together they went on.

They walked for miles and days and hours and months, all in a single afternoon. The cities were groaning carcasses. Tilted buildings and nests of chain link and glass. Under the constant flurry of ashes like snow was the bounty of the new world. Rubber tires and rat skeletons. Twisted metal and smoldering flesh. All of it was swarming with insects in children's clothes. Their endless chittering and cries of "Food! Hungry!" were nails in their ears.

They tried to keep their heads down but failed:

They saw a little girl eating a dog, a dog that had been long dead.

They saw a boy suckling from a bloated goat, the reddened swollen udder leaking putrid milk down his eager face, a stillborn kid dangling from its hindquarters where it had stalled mid-delivery. The flies formed a buzzing cloak of privacy around them.

Temple gagged and prayed. God ought to be used to bile-stained prayers by now, he thought.

Addy stared at the ground and wept none-too-silently.

They kept walking.

Kept bleeding beneath their makeshift armor.

Kept their heads down and wrapped themselves in mumbled prayers and hopeful incantations.

The fire was warm and lovely. Brilliant orange in contrast to the black that was the night. The moon hung in the far corner over the cliff cities. Its once white face now a bastard scowl caked with soot and tumor. Temple held his hands over the flames. His wedding ring was nearly invisible beneath the grime and crust. In the flicker, their sores wept like crying eyes. "What do you think will be there?" he asked Addy, "When will we find The Untouched City?"

Addy never moved. His arm across his exhausted eyes. The fire highlighted the bugs that toiled in his beard. Shimmering diamonds in tangled brush.

"Something," he answered, "Everything." He dozed as silence stomped into the camp, pissed on the fire, and ordered them to bed.

As Temple closed his eyes, he heard another mumbled word from his friend, "Nothing."

The night chopped the moon in two, and each half slid into the land.

The bloodstained clouds grumbled with growing thunder. Behind them, things fluttered and moved.

The two men slept and dreamed.

In their dreams, they never awoke.

COTTONMOUTH

Monday

Ingrid was standing at the kitchen sink, with her back to the doorway, when the sudden chiming of the doorbell startled her. The dirty glass slipped from her fingers and broke upon contact with the edge of the sink.

She rolled her eyes and sighed, wiping the suds from her hands as she walked away.

"Coming," she called out in a half-whine, grabbing the knob to open the door.

"Yes," she huffed impatiently.

Standing on the stoop was a boy, maybe six years old. His blonde hair plastered to his forehead with sweat. His features were flushed bright pink save for the pale that surrounded his mouth and eyes. His pale blue T-shirt stuck to him like a second skin.

"May I have a glass of water?" he asked, his voice was a rusting thing in an old barn.

Her brow furrowed a little, and he managed a half smile.

"I was playing a few houses down, and I have to get home. I played all afternoon and just, well, I'm thirsty. Can I borrow a drink, please?" he managed to explain through his fidgeting.

"Certainly, do you want to come in?" she invited, with a sweep of the arm that was quite hokey, she realized too late. It seemed lost on the little visitor.

"No, I'll wait. I'm all dirty and sweaty." He smiled again, this time it was an unnatural alien thing that crept across his waxy face.

"Okay. Just a minute." Ingrid went to the kitchen and grabbed a glass from the drainer, went to the refrigerator, poured it nearly to the top with ice water, and closed the door. She walked slower back to the doorway, so as to not spill any.

"Here you go," she handed the boy the beverage. He took it without a word and gulped it down eagerly. He wiped his lips on the back of his sticky arm and handed the glass back to her. "Thanks, Lady." And by the time she opened her mouth to say he was welcome, he was gone.

Tuesday

INGRID AWOKE TO the sound of a lawnmower next door. A nagging rattling cacophony that just would not let up until she gave in and stepped into her slippers, waving a white flag at sleeping in. She stood at the sink and held the mug of coffee in her hands.

She peered out through the slats of the blinds and watched the boy cutting the neighbor's lawn. He was quite handsome for his young age, maybe sixteen years old. Blonde hair that hung well past his lanky shoulders. His arms and chest were literally glistening in the sun. She sipped and watched for a while longer before turning and preparing to make breakfast for herself.

The knocking at the door yanked her out of her daydreams like a hand pulling a child from deep water. She sat the mug down and went to the door. She looked out the peephole and groaned. It was the lawn boy. He had put on his shirt though, the pale blue of it matched his eyes. She tightened the belt on her robe and pulled the neck closed. She opened the door a little and peeked through. "Yes?"

"Hi, Ma'am," he began, looking at his feet and stepping side from side in a nervous manner. "Um... I was cutting the grass over there, and, well, they left for the day, and I was wondering if I could trouble you for a glass of water?" She raised an eyebrow and looked at his face, blasted pink and white around the mouth. Working up to heat exhaustion. "Sure," she said, and closed the door. She went and grabbed a cup from the cupboard, an old Biggie Gulp cup from the Quikmart down the block. She filled it with some ice and water from the fridge and walked it to the door. "Here you go, Take it with you. You can just toss the cup in the recycle bin when you're done. 'kay?"

"You got it. Thanks a lot Miss."

He drank the water in two gulps and licked his lips. Her stomach lurched, and she felt warm inside.

You've been alone too damn long woman.

He was walking back towards the neighboring property around the hedged corner, and like some party trick, he was gone. Ingrid performed her own magic and disappeared back into the house.

Wednesday

SHE SAT ON her sofa reading the newest Hap and Leonard book, listening to the television. Rush Limbaugh was blathering on about his hatred of so and so... she shook her head and went back to the book. A dog began barking across the street. She jumped a good foot off of the seat when the doorbell sounded. "Who the hell?" she muttered, laying the book down and going to the door.

She switched on the light and peered through the hole. It was an old man. Not old, old, more like sixty. He was tall and thin and his skin very tanned. He could have been made of beef jerky were he a shade darker. He looked like leather. A blazing contrast to his pale slacks and the light blue shirt he wore. Too tight and stained with moisture. His pale eyes stared straight ahead as he rang the bell again. She opened the door a crack and looked him in the eyes. They were deep and thirsty.

"Yes?" she asked.

"Howdy, Ma'am, sorry to bother you, but my car is on the fritz about 3 blocks down, and I'm walking to the Quickmart for oil, but I need to take a pill. Could I trouble you for a glass of water?" She stared at him. His sandy thinning hair stuck to his skull. His long-drawn features. The pale that surrounded his lips. She closed the door.

"A minute," she barked as she shuffled to the kitchen. "What are the fucking odds?" she hissed under breath. She brought back the glass of icy water and handed it out to him. "Here you are," she said and retreated back to her station behind the barely open door. He tilted back his head and poured the liquid down his throat, no gulping or sipping, just pouring it like a pitcher into a glass. He popped his head back up into its natural state and handed her glass back. "Thanks." He turned and sauntered down the walk until the shadows devoured him. Ingrid felt a touch of revulsion as she looked at the glass and thought of the way he drank it. It made her think of a PEZ dispenser.

Thursday

THE RED NUMBERS said it was 3:19 A.M. when the light tapping awoke her from her sleep. She sat up and shook her head. She didn't bother with a robe, her breasts barely contained by the tank top she wore. She pulled on her sweatpants that were laying by the bed and walked out the hall.

Another round of feeble rat-tat-tats at the front door. "This had better be some sort of emerg--" She stopped upon opening the door. The man on her porch was old. Beyond counting old. He was literally a skeleton wrapped in a puckery parchment of skin where the flesh had mutinied and abandoned the ship. The once blue tee hung on him like an old paper bag. His eyes sunken so far back in the sockets they were nearly gone altogether. "I need a drink, please?" he whispered. His rawhide lips were cracked and weeping white fluid.

"Pardon me?" she asked in annoyed disbelief. She felt suddenly cold and anxious. Her skin chilled and crawled.

"I've been dry for so long..." he swallowed and continued, "I get nervous when I sweat." He managed a wheezing chuckle. It sounded like a graveyard breeze. Ingrid pushed the door almost closed. "I'll get you a glass of water, sir. In just a moment, what are you doing out so late?"

He just stared at her, so she turned and went to the kitchen. She opened the fridge and poured the water. Upon sitting the pitcher back on the shelf, she pulled the door closed, but before it closed and the light vanished, she saw:

Saw the old man beside her. Saw his face old as time. Saw him smiling, a large and feral smile, a thing that took up more than half of his face, a smile of long needles and broken mirrors. A smile of bad times and worse, of lies a thousand years old, and truths far worse than that. She gasped and dropped the glass, which shattered on the floor. She pushed the door open, and the light spread its arms. The man was really there, leaning forward. His face close to hers. No breath came from his nose or mouth. His eyes rolled over white. "Thirsty," he hissed. He held a shard of broken glass in each bony hand.

Then the light disappeared.

THE GOING RATE

With the images on the television providing a strobing background, he held the cloth over her little mouth until her breathing slowed. She looked so much like her mother. As he stared at his daughter, Dennis felt the sad smile he wore wither. If it weren't for that bitch, he wouldn't be doing this now. She was the one who had left him with their daughter so she could "find herself." Had abandoned him with a replica of herself, one that called him Daddy — that and a mountain of debt. He sighed and sniffled back the tears that were coming again.

It was a tax month, and this time Dennis had to pay in. He rubbed his eyes and watched the clock. The collector would be by soon. Looking at the bill and the amount owed, he picked up the shears.

He knelt beside the sofa and stared into his sleeping daughter's face. He lightly slapped her cheek and watched for any sign of consciousness. As the normally pink flesh gave way to bright red, with not so much as an eye twitch, he knew he was okay to proceed. He took her small hand in his and folded the fingers, allowing only the pinky to remain extended. Holding it between his thumb and finger, he slid it between the blades. He closed his eyes and ground his teeth hard enough to taste the enamel. The bones snapped with a small crack. The girl winced but did not wake. Thank God for sedatives. He grabbed the ice pack beside him and held it against the slightly spurting nub, then took the shoelace and tied off the base of the finger as tightly as he could. He looked at the iron sitting on the table beside him, wavery lines of heat rising from it, waiting to cauterize.

He picked up the finger and wrapped it in the proper form, stuffed it into the red envelope, and went to the porch. The porch lights winked on one at a time. There were three lights crying red.

He slid the clear pane from the light box and swapped it for a red panel of glass, the one he kept in the decorative milk box by the door.

At the far end of the street, a shadow broke free. A long shape that took on more detail as it stretched to the center of the roadway. Dennis stepped back into the house, closing the door. He peered through curtains as the taxman approached.

Tall as time and as long as hours, it strode down Main Street. Cloven feet clicking like boot heels on asphalt. Its fish-belly skin glistened like fungi under the full moon. A black suit, stitched with black hole and strychnine. The taxman's arms ended in hands like squid. Impossible fingers, like lengths of living rope. The taxman stopped at old man Ordini's house where he stepped onto the porch, knelt, and picked up the red envelope from the mat. The thing swiveled in the direction of Dennis's house and smiled at him. The smile was stitches and railroad ties. The eyes that nested above it were beetles in cataract flesh. Dennis felt his bowels somersault.

The taxman tore open the parcel and extracted something red and dripping. He ate it, reached into the mailer, and with a

106

bloody finger, drew a large circle on the door. The light went out on the porch, and the taxman was back in the street.

Dennis shook as he watched it collect its wages. A tongue from the Melvoins. Mrs. Dib owed something small. Old man Mellick must have owed more than anyone, for his envelope bulged so, a slender hand dangling from the unsealed end.

Dennis closed his eyes, and when he opened them, the thing stood on his stoop. Its face inches from his, only glass and curtain fabric between them. The eyes were bottomless. Reminding him of the dark and fetid water of the sinkhole on his grandfather's farm. He sighed and slid down the wall to sit on the floor. He could not bear to watch this thing eat his little girl's finger. To see its face up close was almost enough to shred his mind. His wife had always done the taxes. She was the one who knew the ins and outs, not him. He heard a scraping noise as the thing drew the circle on the door. He could smell the rich scent of the blood. Then, the clip-clop of hooves on the sidewalk.

Had he still had a tongue, he'd have screamed.

DOWN BY THE OCEAN

A million pebbles beneath booted feet. One for every prayer unanswered from now on. The sky was a pale puzzle missing pieces. The clouds sagged, and the tears danced down upon us. We stood in a large circle around the thing. The entire village populace, and still the damned thing was bigger.

It had washed ashore during the night, as had many things over the years. Crilly was located far enough down the coast to serve as a sort of sieve for the ocean currents. Dead whales, dolphins, squid, sometimes dead people had all found their way upon our rocky shore. This was something entirely different. Quite alien.

A large white mass. Alabaster and sinuous, it smelled of salt and sea and carried an underlying scent, unique. Sickly sweet. Its wet skin glistened in the feeble sunlight. We watched the birds dart and hover. The scavenger gulls wouldn't even land on it. They shrieked and danced in the air.

"Queer," Hardy grumbled, pulling down his cap and hunching his shoulders. "I think it may be a whale, long dead and bleached by the sun. Had her innards ett by the sea, this is just the husk, I think." He stepped close and stopped short of actually touching it. He wrinkled his nose, and a look of strange unease skittered across his face. His gray bush of a beard appeared to bristle as he looked away.

"Not. I think it's a giant squid. I see stumps of tentacle, I see lumps of insides. I see a big dead eye," Bitch Hattie chirped, and she chewed on the stub of a cigar between her crooked teeth.

The village, we stood and stared at the odd thing. We were about to return to the warmth of our homes when we saw the movement. This unnatural thing billowed like a balloon. A fleshy parachute caught in a tree. A dying jellyfish under the shadow of a foot. All those things.

"See that?" asked Vicar Marsh.

"Just gas. Or maybe some eels or fish, what got trapped in its body," Hardy barked. He spat a lunger onto the stones, the blood and yellow of it shining like a precious gem. He wiped his mouth on his sleeve. He leaned and picked up a large board that had washed up as well. He stepped forward and poked the carcass. Seawater foamed from the dimpled flesh, and he gagged at the wave of stench that assaulted him.

He thought he heard laughter and stood statue straight. "Marsh, ya hear it?" he gasped.

"I do," was all he got as an answer. The lanky minister stepped forward and bowed closer to the leviathan. The rest of the villagers shuffled forward and leaned, the whoosh of the waves and the cries of the gulls were all I heard. A minute later, even those sounds stopped.

There was a low growling sound coming from the elephantine body on the beach. Little Timmy Farmer toddled forward and smiled as he touched the thing. Smacking the milky flesh with his tiny hand.

Fast as lightning. The flesh billowed into the air, a cape of rotting offal. Blacking out the sun. Being the farthest back, I stumbled and rolled to the foot of the dune. I cowered and watched. The thing was beyond comprehension. A living skeleton, three oar-lengths in height. It was covered in eyes and mouths. Where there were no eyes or mouths, tentacles sprouted and waved about. Several of the arms sprouted smaller creatures that were merely heads with mouths full of razored fang. They stretched and choked and captured the villagers. It pulled them to it. The carcass that had concealed the thing was now a roiling and spasming pouch of sorts, it bulged behind it and served as stomach for what it caught in its wiggling limbs. Bitch Hattie screamed and turned to flee. A tentacle caught her wooden leg and splintered it off at the thigh. She teetered and fell only to be drawn into the maw of the horror. Her sandpaper screams rising like black balloons.

I pressed myself flatter against the dune and pulled sand up over myself. I could not stop whimpering and hoped to elude its attention. I burrowed under as far as I could and lay still.

Then the feeding frenzy was over. The monster drew up into itself, coiling up like a chrysalis. It rolled itself into the surf, and the pale fleshy flap that served as stomach and camouflage now acted as sail as it swallowed the breeze and sailed it out to sea. I stayed where I lay, piss soaked and sandy. Raw eyed and voiceless.

And as I stood on shaking legs and took in the bloody scene before me, all I could think of was the story of the Trojan horse.

A FEE FOR FABLES

ts movements were graceful yet jerky in a way, perhaps like a spasming man underwater might look. Every movement had a soundtrack of whisper; the papery skin making contact with another patch of papery skin. In the dimness of dusk, it appeared to be made of hornet nest. Crepe of dusty gray and threaded with black.

The only buzzing was the sound of her heart as she lay in bed and peered through the space between the bottom of the blind and the window ledge. Her nightgown sticking to her sweat-sheened skin. The whisper-skinned thing walked around out at the edge of the yard. Its bulbous head nodded slightly, and its too-long neck seemed to struggle to keep it upright.

It turned, and though she couldn't tell if it had eyes, seemed to gaze right at her window, directly into her room. Her breath hitched, and she held a gasp behind small teeth. It held up an arm that ended in an appendage with only two long digits, one of which it jammed upwards in a swift and unexpected motion, impaling the lower part of its face. Then, with another flurry of movement, dragged the inserted finger sideways, tearing a ragged

113

wound in its face. The wound opened, bits of the mache-like flesh dangling or dancing away on the light breeze. The corners rose as it smiled. Black things shined and wriggled within. Beetle backs and static squirming. It seemed to stare right at Marcy's window, tilting that large head forward to exaggerate the fact it might be looking into her paling face.

She lay as still as possible. Not breathing or blinking. She heard a voice flutter through the screen of the window. It was a small thing of moth wings and blowing sand that said, "I know you see..."

Marcy woke with the sun and pulled the blanket over her face, not the whole way, just to the bridge of her nose. A modern Kilroy. The aroma was both comforting and slightly repulsive: sour perspiration, something slightly salty and acidic stitched to another smaller fungal reek. She breathed deep and embraced the fragrances with sighing lungs. A wheezing and cracking bones symphony when she moved to sit upright. Movement at the window drew her attention. Marcy felt her pulse quicken, and she went cold. She slowly peered out into the yard, and with relief, found it was only the crow out there again. It stood on the sill and tapped the glass three times and disappeared. Her heart replies in kind from within its cage of weakened ribs and sagging skin. Another sigh, and the blankets were tossed aside, a womb torn apart to leave her vulnerable and raw.

There is no crueler thing to do but get up and face another day.

In the husk of the kitchen, Marcy sits and takes another sip of the brown in the chipped mug. She cannot taste it. Her tongue tingles and dances as the memory of words and speech skulk upon it. She's been alone for so very long. She hears a soft voice by her ear, *"I know you see me."*

114

She feels the tear run down her cheek as she struggles to decide whether it was a recollection of the dream or vision she had last night, or a plea with the world to just acknowledge she exists. She decides it's both, and words begin to trickle from her mouth:

"Consequence is this old ratty string around my finger, hardened by the dried sweat and saliva of days or weeks.

"I chew on it anyway, this jerkied life.

"I felt the stale fetuses of repercussions grind and mash between molar and gum.

"I swallowed and felt them grow in my belly.

"When not stillborn, they might've been beautiful monsters.

"That was my hope.

"I ought to also have known better,

"I have shoeboxes under my bed.

"Filled with the brittle bones of hope,

"as delicate as a dead bird.

"I fill my hands with them sometimes at night,

"rub them along the flesh of my jaw.

"Smooth and sharp at the same time.

"Like words that smell like teeth."

Marcy raises the mug to her lips and bites its edge with slightly crooked teeth. She feels the ceramic against enamel, and it makes her spine shiver a bit. Her jaw clamps a little harder and hears the vessel crack and feels the bits stick to her teeth and lips. Marcy places it on the table and looks at the chipped spot along the top edge, then to its twin on the other side of the mug. She wipes her mouth with her hand and stands. Marking X's on a calendar would be easier.

"The moon smiles in the window when I'm not looking. The moment I turn to catch it, the smile swerves into sneer, and the

night goes out. I'm not bothered. The best darkness is the absolute kind."

Marcy watches the red numbers of the clock as they change, each minute dying with a silent dignity. She rolls closer to the window and grips the bottom of the blind between her crooked fingers, raising it slightly, slowly. The shed stands at the far corner, bathed in silver moonlight. The dried corn stands tilted and stooped in the garden that died of neglect. She feels a tingle in her shoulder when she notes movement from the corner of her view. The thing moves into her line of sight with sure but slow steps. She squints and notes the differences a day makes. The braided sash of dark hair that hangs from its shoulders and neck like Jacob Marley's sins. It comes as close as the edge of the garden before stopping. Marcy stares at her visitor for long minutes that sting like hours. It makes no movements, no gestures. Just quietly staring and daring. Marcy rolls away from the window to take a bottle of pills from her nightstand. She swallows two and gulps the last of the tap water in the glass that has been there for a week. She closes her eyes and tries to remember the fable that her sentinel reminded her of before the herd of slumber tramples her down.

Her bones ache a little more than usual. She worries that maybe she had walked in her sleep and fallen. The bruises on her calves and the back of her arm are dark plum and just as tender. She winces as she strokes them.

"Better be more careful, old girl."

She empties the last of the shredded wheat into the bowl and eats it without milk. Expiration dates always break her heart. She crunches and stares at the black phone mounted on the wall, covered in dust, while behind her tired eyes she sees rivers and boats. It is only as she approaches her mouth with the last piece of cereal that she notices her fingernails are the color of bruises. She sighs and finishes her breakfast. It's the most important meal of the day.

Marcy sits on the porch, her sentinel appearing just before eleven. She sips at her glass of water and watches as it paces the edges of her property. Bits of its papery skin dancing on the breeze, whispered muttering dancing from its mouth. Marcy finishes her water and rocks quietly for a moment. The being stands still at the foot of the porch steps and looks up at the old woman. The mouth bent upward into a smile of sorts. She sees it has eyes now, but realizes they are a pair of wasps sitting idle on either side of its head. It doesn't move, and the breeze dies, and all she can hear is the oceanic whispering beneath its skin. She feels the buzz within again and it begins to rise like a tide. She closes her eyes and sees churning waters, sees a thin, pale hand, and hears the clinking of chains...of change. She stands and goes inside.

It is early evening when Marcy returns to the porch. The creature has not moved at all, it still stands at the base of the steps. Marcy sighs and smiles, squinting up to the sky as she does so.

"All these days, I knew it but didn't. I kept thinking of stories. Of rhymes and tales. Poetic portents that I paid no attention to. I nearly didn't put it together. When you get old, you get ignorant. Or maybe we start that way and just idle, willfully so. You fill your head with stories your whole life and never once realize that there's a fee to be paid. A life poorly written is a life unlived. A life spent alone is a diary entry of the lonely doomed."

Marcy steps down closer to the thing, and it tilts its head toward her. Is it nodding? That wound of a smile moving slightly. It holds out its right arm, the hand at the end of it open and waiting. Marcy holds out a gnarled hand of her own and opens it, two coins falling to land in the upturned palm of her visitor.

Everything stills, and Marcy releases the breath she's been holding for so very long. She opens her eyes and finds her creature gone.

"The neighbor was on her walk and noticed the flies. She called it in. Said she hadn't seen the old bird in a few days," the young man in the white uniform blathers.

"Her name was Marcy Oates, and I'd put it as at least a week, maybe more like two." The red-faced man's eyes are rimmed with wet.

"Did you know her?" the other man asks, a tint of shame across his features.

"No, I'm just the sensitive type," Red Face snaps, a little snottier than needed. The two slowly roll the old woman from the bed where she's been laying for some time. Her flesh is blue and purple and splitting in spots. The sheets stained dark in their mourning ruin. Flies buzz to get at their squirming brood.

"Marcy Oates," Red Face mumbles again as he scribbles on the pad in his hand.

"Natural causes, looks like," the other man chimes in.

Red Face nods and flips his tablet closed and gets back to trying to wrangle the body into the vinyl bag and onto the stretcher. They manage to get her out the front door and down the steps before Red Face stops. His eyes are stuck on the two coins laying in the dead grass in front of the bottom step.

INTRUDER

The clouds are like thumbprint smudges on dark glass. I pull my zipper tighter, put the hood up, and stay close to the buildings that edge the alley. I like that the places I choose are within walking distance. I like the fact that I know these people, some mere passing acquaintances, others close neighbors and friends. Almost like it's my neighborhood, and I do as I like.

I'm counting my steps by twos, up to nearly three hundred, when I see the garage that I marked earlier that day. All the damn houses in this development look the same. Cookie-cuttery eyesores straight outta 80's Spielberg. Once the sun disappears, it's too easy to become disoriented, so I marked it with a small dab of mud. A tiny dot above the center window in the garage door. Dot marks the spot. I lick my thumb and wipe the mud from the white aluminum, then I duck around the building to the waiting path. I'm at twenty-four steps by the time I reach the gate.

The metal is chilled by the autumn night. I feel it through my gloves. I pull the latch back and step inside the yard. I am up to ten when I stop in my tracks. Did I latch the gate? I walk backward, counting backward by twos until I am reacquainted with *numero two-O*. The gate is latched. Dammit. I start again. I make it nearly to the side porch before the nagging begins again. The gate is not latched. Sure it is, I already checked it. Did I? I'm positive. My forehead is sweating, and I'm starting to shake a little. Fuck me. I step off the deck and walk back through the yard, counting and cursing simultaneously. I had latched the gate. You down with OCD? Yeah, you know me! I line up her trash cans in a perfect row before I go back toward the house. I carefully unscrew the bulb from the porch light. I can pick the lock easily enough without illumination. I had memorized all of the *Time Life Home Repair* books by the time I was six. I'm an unsung master at wiring and locks, plumbing and heating, windows and doors. I can also tell you the model name and number of your ceiling fan, faucets, and microwave at a glance.

I slip inside. The house is immaculate, not enough for someone like me, but far from what a normal person would consider a mess. I adjust the light on my headband and turn it on. My gaze follows the soft beam as I take in the kitchen. Three tall chairs, a butcher block table. On the table is a large purse, a handful of change, sixty-seven cents, actually. Keys, a cell phone, and a pack of cinnamon gum. I turn to make my way through the house and stop dead. On the counter beside the sink is a plate with a partially eaten sandwich on it, a soiled fork, and an empty glass with lipstick on its edge. I feel nausea begin to boil in my stomach. Repulsed, I close my eyes and begin to count. By threes. I throw the partial sandwich away and turn the water on, barely above a trickle, to wash the items. I make no sound when placing them in the strainer or drying my hands. I put the lid down on the trash bin on my way out of the room.

INTRUDER

The living room is large and tidy. All the times I stood out front and talked while I delivered the mail, I never would have guessed the home was this spacious. The room holds a sofa, a couch, two bookshelves, a chair, and two end tables. On one of the tables, there is a stack of catalogs and periodical propaganda, which is stacked incorrectly, all the spines to one side. This makes the pile slide in an untidy manner. I sigh through my nose and fix them, intermittently alternating the spines to keep the pile level and neat. That completed, I refold the throw blankets and arrange the pillows by size on the sofa. I align all the rugs symmetrically with the walls. I straighten all of the papers on the desk. I organize her CDs and DVDs, put her books into their proper order on the shelves. I straighten the lampshades and all the pictures on the walls precisely. All without making a sound. I sit down and give my roaring nerves a brief rest. In my head, I recite William Burroughs' "Thanksgiving Prayer." It is exactly 1:13 a.m. I approach the stairs. I start counting.

Her bedroom door is open just a crack. The air smells of her soap and shampoo and skin. I turn off the light on my head and peer into the cavernous room. The faint moonlight that has managed to escape its cloudy bonds splashes the walls in an eerie glow. I've always found the woman lying on the bed beautiful, but tonight, she is breathtaking. She sleeps soundly, her little snores like bees buzzing, filling the room. Her skin is as smooth as china and nearly as white. Paper doll white. Her black hair spreads out around her like a spray of blood. I resist the urge to punch her sleeping face as hard as I can. I fight the impulse to lean down and kiss her. To bite and swallow her cheeks. I stand and stare.

Thirty-seven seconds later, I smile and go to my next destination.

The bathroom is at the end of the hall. I close the door and slowly open the sink cabinet. I find certain items and set them atop the Formica counter, next to the brushes and combs. I pull down my pants and groom my pubic hair with her combs and brushes. I clench my hands into tight fists, four times. I squeeze my eyes tight with each clench and exhale deeply. I open them and get to work. I dull all of her razors with soap. I pour bathroom cleaner into her shampoo and conditioner. I put astringent into her mouthwash. I use her deodorant on my taint. I sit on her toilet and stick her toothbrush up my asshole and color the rim with her lipstick. Pull my pants up. I go through her medicine cabinet and note the contents. I can tell by her meds that she's hopelessly crazy. Before I go, I put a pinhole in her diaphragm and re-hang her toilet paper the correct way, with the end facing out.

I navigate the staircase in total darkness. Counting every step. Fourteen from the bathroom to her bedroom door, another ten from that doorway to the landing. Eighteen from the landing down the stairs to the living room. I unplug her phone and everything else in the room. Two-four-six-eight-ten-twelve-fourteen-Kitchen-Ho!

I bend the tines on all of her forks. Put salt in her sugar bowl and fill her salt shaker with sugar. I open the fridge and start in on the contents. I pour out her pitcher of ice water and refill it with white vinegar. I loosen the lids on all of the jars and bottles in the kitchen: syrups, sauces, spices, jellies, and jams. All of them. Leaving them *just* tight enough to allow her to pick them up. I stick straight pins into her apples and pears. I use one of the needles to puncture her eggs and empty them of yolk and white.

My problem is that I'm always thinking. Dredging up years' worth of trivia about rock musicians, movies, sports, and history.

I hear song lyrics while I'm talking myself out of stabbing the counter girl at the coffee shop in the face. I recite biblical psalms while watching pornography. I run through the contents of manuals and books while I walk my route each day. I can smile and shake your hand, stuff letters in your hungry mail slot, all while ranking serial killers by geographical location and body count or alphabetically. There is always too much noise and interference. A dull static, peppered with errant voices. Swatches of songs and movie dialogue. An enormous mural of fresh paint in a rainstorm, it's a runny garish mess. Did I mention this is all the time? While counting or twitching or planning or sleeping. Shitting or pissing or working or fucking or whatever. My mind never stops. Even now, I'm working out next week's schedule in my head. Crazy. I used to try to make sense of the droning rhetoric in my skull. Now I just seize random commands that fly by and file them away so I may act on them later, and I'm a happier camper for it. I think.

I hear a creak above me and stop - stone still. A minute crawls by, then another, and another. Nothing. I exhale and step toward the door. My foot bumps something and I look down to find a pile of shoes beside the door frame. Flip flops, a pair of boots, ratty sneakers, and a pair of black shoes. I sigh and breathe out through my nostrils loudly. Disdainfully. She's a pig. I bend and align the footwear, heel to wall, straight and paired. I fill with warmth as I stand. I take a piece of gum from her pack upon the table and slip out and into the night, stealthy as shadow.

From porch to gate, I count by fours on the exit route. I'm near the end of the alley when I stop and sigh. I didn't latch the gate. I try to resist the need to turn and go back and make sure. The pressure that is always in my chest increases like there's an exploding landmine trapped inside. My eyes begin to water and sweat oozes from all pores.

"Sonofabitch," I snarl softly and creep back down the alley to find the gate latched. Keeping to the shrouded side of the alley, I make my way home.

I get nearly two blocks before I have to go back and check that fucking gate again.

THE PASS

Wayne was anxious to get out of that warehouse. The smells made his head hurt, but then he got outside, and the scents out there did the same. A bitter trade of paint fumes and burning metal for rotting trash and apathy. At least the day was over. Wayne set about cutting through the Sheds on his way home from work, just like he did every night after his shift ended. He worked at the C.H. Lucia Trucking hub as a sorter/loader. The building was a monster of steel, sheet metal, and concrete that was indiscernible from the other metal, steel, and concrete beasts in the heart of the "Sheds." That's what the local nickname for the expansive industrial park was. Wayne looked around and sighed as a wave of nostalgia washed over him.

When Wayne was a kid, this had been called "The Woods," an area of trees that separated the shopping centers and eating establishments from the apartment complexes and housing developments. The Woods was a small haven for the wildlife that had been forced out of their habitat with the encroachment of modern society. Every time they tore down a copse of trees or burned the brush and high grass to throw up some pressboard and vinyl abomination, the animals would crowd here.

By the time he was in his second year of college, the woods were gone and all that remained was the park, which was really just a small cluster of trees and a few benches made from recycled plastic bags. These were presented by the local grocery companies, in grotesque irony. Wayne stomped his way between huge trucks and reeking dumpsters, across oil-stained macadam and broken glass. He stopped suddenly when he realized that the park was gone now as well. He felt like Iron Eyes Cody for a moment, then continued homeward.

He rounded the corner of what used to be Jade Chinese Buffet, long closed down. The owner died and the business had folded, but if you asked locals, you got varying tales of inspections where they found cats in the freezer, to the story that they were trapping rats and rabbits in the back lot and using them as meat in their dishes. The sun slipped behind the looming billboards and cast long tree-like shadows across his path. The closest to a real tree you'd get around here. Wayne pulled a pack of crackers from his jacket pocket and began to munch as he walked. He was beat and would sleep well tonight.

The fawn stood out against its drab urban background, a drop of blood in a glass of milk. It was so small and frail. It stood right in front of him, no more than twelve feet away. The light made it look almost transparent. The spots that mottled its light fur seemed to ripple in the dusk. "Hey," Wayne whispered, and the animal tilted its head in his direction. Wayne took a cracker, crumbled it, and laid the dusty crumbs on the ground. He took a few steps backward and waited.

The deer came forward and bent to eat the offering. Wayne felt a sense of giddiness as the smile threatened to split his face. Where did this little thing come from? There were no woods around anymore. He had a million questions as he watched its little pink tongue snake out and lap up the cracker crumbs. It stood upright and looked into Wayne's eyes, and he felt it. An immense sense of hurt which filled him like a blister. He looked down and saw the cracker pieces just where he left them and as soon as he looked at the fawn again, he understood why. The deer had wandered over in front of the dumpster where it grazed on a patch of weeds that had defiantly forced their way through the cracks in the pavement. As the animal chewed, the weeds stood still in the breezeless air. The word WASTE was painted in large white letters on the front of the skip, letters he was reading *through* the fawn like looking through a fish tank. His breath stopped for a moment, and like his breath, the fawn was quickly gone.

Wayne was shaking and sweating, his perception seemed all wrong. He wasn't sure what was happening. He began to walk faster. He half-jogged down the block towards his building. His eyes widened as he discovered his path was blocked by a school of fish swimming through the air, about four feet above the ground. Big round eyes and swishing tails as they swam in a waterless stream. A water snake the size of a child's arm cut a swath through the school of fish towards the telephone pole that marked the corner. The faded remnants of several yard sale signs seemed to ripple in the phantom current. Wayne stood still for a moment. His mind raced with a thousand thoughts, not many rational. He cut down the alley behind the McDonald's and approached the front of his building. There stood a huge oak tree, its branches literally sagging with birds. Owls, hawks, and eagles, cardinals, and blue jays... so many types and so many birds it was as though the branches bristled with feathered leaves. There were at least a dozen vultures perched on the wrought-iron fencing that lined the street, craning slender necks and pink sagging flesh accented their accusatory gazes. Ghostly opossums waddled along the curb. Across the street, he saw spectral bears dancing and playing between the rows of shining cars at the auto dealership. Over by the trash cans that lined the curb, silvery beavers built a dam of phantom branches.

His pores seemed to be gushing, and his stomach was jumpy and nervous, though these things seemed to pose no physical threat to him. His head was thrumming with a whining sound. He ached in his bones, a deep sorrowful ache. A funeral feeling. With jittery fingers, he shoved the key into the lock and turned it, and as it clicked, the world stopped. His ears filled with the chatter of locusts and the keening of crickets. He smelled fresh air and cold water, pine needles and soil. A crow's caw hooking behind his eyes. He looked around, and every ghost of every animal he had encountered lined the street behind him. Cars drove through them unaware, and the streetlights hummed and illuminated them all. They sat or stood as statues and watched Wayne open the door. He could almost make out the shadowy wilderness that stood in the same space as the buildings of the block. His eyes were wet, and his vision blurred. He could not explain the primal sadness he was feeling, the lump in his throat that threatened to stop his breath. He pushed open the door and slipped inside, locking it behind him. A sob escaping like a gust of flame.

The world and the night continued on.

THIS TWILIGHT GARDEN

The lot was hedged with thick shrubs and squat bushes. Where there were gaps, there was a fence. Nice, tall, plank fence. Miller stared up at the moon with wet eyes and spoke quietly to no one. He picked up the spade and knelt beside the garden. A small rectangle of tilled earth adjacent to the unused garage. He gouged and turned the soil and watched the dislodged worms as they squirmed and wriggled back into hiding. He swiveled and took one handle of the black cargo bag that sat on the grass. He unzipped it and took out his newest trophy.

The pale green silk of the handkerchief had darkened from the blood that soaked it. He looked at the heart in the moonlight, a fist of glistening black muscle. It had held all of her love. He gently placed it in the furrow and covered it with dirt. He picked up the small marker he had made, a ruler-sized sliver of wood with a name written upon it in flowing cursive. This one was Emily. She had actually kissed him. Her lips dry and trembling, tasting of fruit flavored wax. He picked up the watering can and sprinkled its contents over the tiny mound, as well as the six other marked mounds and their name stakes...

Mary, the one who had held his hand.

Thelma, the tall girl with the birthmark over her ear. She talked to him for hours, but never listened.

Carrie, plain and sweet but so full of self-loathing. Sara, the dark-haired dirty girl, her eager hands were her downfall.

Alice, she wanted money and fame and was gone as soon as it was made clear Miller could supply neither.

Patricia, the quiet girl. She smiled and listened and did all the right things, but in the end, she was not the one.

His knees popped as he stood and looked at the garden and the markers. It was like a miniature cemetery. He went back into the house to get something to eat and to prepare for his evening.

Loneliness is a lot like a too-big room or ill-fitting clothes. These girls. These girls were loved by him but at some point sought to leave him. They all broke his heart. He knew it was not their fault. The heart is a seed. It can only grow as much as the hull will allow, and if the seed is damaged or sick, then it will grow monstrous and wrong. If you love something, set it free...

He decided to free the seeds and plant anew. He stood at the kitchen window and watched the moonlight soak his garden. And as he chewed, he saw the ripples in the soil. Small rolling waves. He saw the fingers as they sprouted from the earth and reached towards the sky. He saw the arms extend. They were growing. He saw the arms and heads break through the earth, the moonlight painted dusty breasts silver. It was working. My God, it was working!

He sat at the table and straightened his tie. Seven heart-shaped boxes of candy and seven single roses waited on the wooden surface. He heard muffled groans and the sound of bare feet on patio tile. The cloying smell of earth and something deeper was coming through the window screen. He licked his fingers, smoothed down his hair, and wished he had a mint.

SUMMER GULLET

They stood before the hole: Stiggy, Donny, and Joanie. The three musketeers in black leather and torn denim. The sky was fading to a dull pumpkin orange, and the wind had slowed to an almost nonexistent whisper. The smell still hung over the pit before them. It was a completely unique odor, thick and sticky. A multitude of carnival fragrances: cotton candy, corn dogs, fry oil and sugar and salty sweat - all wrapped together in a funky burrito of stench that was dancing from the yawning chasm before them. Underneath those nostalgic scents was something dank and sinister; mud and rot and something unsettlingly organic. Behind them, the skeleton of the rollercoaster loomed like a sleeping dinosaur. The derelict Ferris wheel was a blind eye. Bats dove and whipped about the dead lights that hung from bird-shit crusted wires. The trio paid no attention to any of this, they were staring at the hole.

Stiggy reached down and picked up a large chunk of brick that was lying next to his foot. He tossed it into the pit. They all leaned forward and listened for it to hit the bottom, and Joanie grimaced as she looked into the thing. It was like an enormous mouth. Toothless but hungry. The walls were wet and bright, swirled with garish colors. Pink and blue. Gold and brilliant red. In addition to the stinking breeze rising from below were sounds. A cacophony of calliope music, screams and laughter, the occasional shard of rock music... bands like Journey and Styx, Buttrock bands was what their pal Chadder had called them, that were popular that last summer before the park closed. Underneath those sounds, something very low - a coarse rumbling - an animal growling deeply in its throat or a stomach betraying its hunger. Or the slight hiss of scales on stone. The amplified rattling of bones. The last wheeze of exhausted lungs.

Stiggy straightened his posture and stepped back a little. "So, what do you think?" he asked his cronies. They continued staring into the abyss. It was Donny who first offered his answer.

"What the hell, dude? Maybe a sinkhole. Park's been shut up for like three years now." His voice was quivering slightly, like he was very nervous. He looked like a scared little boy, aside from the lion's mane of permed wooly hair that framed his features. Tiny blue eyes darted like gnats.

"It's like a big mouth. A big lipless toothless mouth." Joanie whispered, her uneasy gaze never straying from that gaping maw at their feet. She looked at Donny, his earlobe. She did not like this at all. A shiver climbed her spine, an invisible marsupial.

"When did you find it?" Donny asked. He kicked a dented soda can until it rolled over the edge and into the void. They listened for it to hit the bottom but like the brick, it never did. The only sound was an eerie burst of high-pitched giggling from the bottom of a well. The laughter fluttered about them like moths.

"I was here last week. That night Gina pissed me off. I either needed to walk off some anger or put my fist through her damn teeth. So, I decided that walking off some anger was probably the best choice." Stig spat onto the dusty ground, licked his lips, and continued. "So, I was walking around here because it's quiet and creepy, and I dig that. I was over by that ticket who was tugging at the pewter skull that dangled from the booth takin' a piss when I heard laughing... a kid laughing. So, I zip up and come to see who it was, and there was this big hole here. I yelled down, I thought maybe some kid fell in there. I don't know. Nothing. No answer, but it smells... this hole." He pauses and studies the faces of his friends. They stare like a hypnotist's audience. "Like summertime. Like years ago, summertime. Candy and fun and sweating and laughing and eating... the sounds were down there too, roller coasters clunking and carousel music and rocking music shit from the Whippit Ride... I even heard people doin' it'... all kinds a weird shit." Stig paused and jammed his hands further into his pockets. The tip of his pinky poked from a ragged hole in the denim like a grub.

"I must've zoned out a bit, and when I snapped out of it, I was almost ready to fall the hell in. I was leaning so far over it. It creeped me out, and I left... fast. But I been thinkin' about it ever since."

Stig stood very still and looked at the other two. "I think it's a grave, yeah, I think that's what I think." Donny and Joanie looked at him with arched eyebrows.

"It's alive," Donny stammered. "A living grave, how is that?" They stared and listened. As they did so, the night sky darkened as the stars began to wink out in surrender, handing all attention to the moon.

"It's where summers and childhood go when they die," Stig clarified. "That's what I think." He stepped closer to the edge. A faint mist began creeping from the mouth of the hole like smoke machine funhouse fog. There was the clunky sound of bumper cars colliding... squeals... giggles... the guitar riff from "You Shook Me All Night Long." Stig snaked an arm into the mist and touched the inner wall of the pit. It was warm and moist and pulsing. He withdrew and licked his fingertips. They tasted like caramel covered apples. He looked up at his friends with tearing eyes. "I'm not sure how something that ain't really living can die." The encroaching shadow was splintered by strobing beams from the pit, which pulled back into it, like some disco proboscis.

"This is it," he swallowed thickly. "This is where it goes. When we trade in our fun cards for time cards. Hand over our cool clothes for monkey suits, uniforms, or business casual. Go from rock and roll to whatever shit our geezer parents are diggin'. We sacrifice ourselves a little at a time without realizing it... until we are just plain gone!" He wiped his nose on a denim sleeve. The smear it left was shiny as glass. "We watch as we slit our own throats with an endless piece of paper, and we do it over and over again!" Tears were running from his squinting, angry eyes.

"You're sounding nuts, man!" Donny stated, and he took a step back, his leather jacket crinkled as he hugged himself. Stig looked at him. It was a hard look. Donny went on: "That doesn't make a lick of sense. I mean, I don't wanna grow up and sell out any more than you. But you're sounding a little, I don't know, looney!" Joanie just kept staring into the hole.

"Am I?" Stiggy had barely spoken the words when he charged and caught him by surprise, grabbing Donny around the arms and neck. "I can't go like that... can you?" he shouted as they scuffled.

Joanie covered her eyes. Donny shrieked as Stig gained the advantage and footing. With little effort, he hurled the screaming boy into the pit. The giggles and laughter grew in pitch until they morphed into ragged howls and wet ripping sounds. Stig looked at Joanie, a wormy smile taking over his face. She shook her head and backed away. She was much easier to take than Donny was. She was lighter too.

Stig sat on the edge of the pit. Legs dangling, the hole's slithering tongues caressed his calves with their spun sugar stickiness. The flesh sizzled wherever they touched. He did not care. In his mind, it was summer. Girls were strutting, and the park was alive. School was a hundred years away. He was seventeen again. Still. Always. He pushed off the edge like a swimmer into a pool. The carnival below grew louder yet; at its loudest, it could not drown out his screams.

TINSEL

very stood on the stoop as the wind and snow swirled around him. His cheeks were raw yet hot, even in this weather. The frigid sting of the cold was welcome.

He slipped the key into the lock, and with a turn, he was inside. Leaning back against the door, he drew a deep breath. The house still smelled like Marie, that faint flowery smell of her shampoo, the powder-diffused tang of sweat emanating from the recliner. He took a slow visual tour of the living room and basking in all the memories there — the basket beside the chair, the crossword puzzle book that still lay open to the page she was working on when she had the stroke, the barrister bookcase...

They were in their twenties when she spotted the bookcase from across the parking lot at the flea market. Dark mahogany, etched glass in the pull doors...it was beautiful. Over the years, her nimble fingers must have danced countless times over every nick and scrape along its aged veneer.

"How much?" she had asked that day, with her bubbly giggle so lovely.

The man behind the counter removed the cigarette from his cracked lips to answer: "Two hundred. That's an antique."

Avery held out his hand, Marie took it, and they made to walk away.

"I can take a hundred, just so I don't gotta lug the damn thing back on the truck."

They stopped and smiled at one another, proud of their charade's success.

"Sold!"

Now it sat in the corner of the living room, as it had for these last fifty years. Half a century worth of books and gewgaws. Worn, pulp paperbacks and hardcovers had long ago filled it to capacity. The piece now stood nearly hidden behind stacks of books and magazines.

Avery sighed and dropped his wool coat on the floor. "Hang it up, Ave," he could almost hear Marie holler as he went to the kitchen.

Fifty-seven years with the woman. A lifetime.

They had met when he was twenty. Marie, a clerk at the Save-U-Mor, and Avery, a long-haired hood who worked at The Sound Pound, a record shop next door. When shopping, he would make a point of going to her register, telling her stupid jokes. She pretended not to find him amusing. He asked her out but made it sound like she was doing him a favor. She accepted but disguised it as a pitiful gesture.

They saw *Night of the Living Dead* and had a great time, so they went out again. Love notes clipped to timecards, under windshield wipers, roses on car seats. He once gave her a bottle of rain. With Marie, a mundane trip to the grocery store was a loving adventure. The years fluttered by like birds.

Until now.

Avery heated up a can of chicken soup and set a steaming bowl of it down on the only clear spot on the dinner table. Staring ahead, he slowly sipped the broth.

All the mail from the week — bills, junk mail, newspapers — sat in a heap beside him. There were pencils and pens, a pile of clipped coupons, a roll of paper towels, a dismantled cuckoo clock he had been fixing for the last three years, a Mason jar full of pennies. He shook his head and smiled. "How ever did you tolerate me, woman?"

Sipping golden broth, it was hard to get it past the lump in his throat.

They had been watching *Jeopardy!* when the stroke hit.

"What is Pygmalion?" she had uttered, followed by a strange noise.

Avery sat with his nose in one of his old pulps. "What?" he responded to the question he assumed she must have asked him. No answer came. After a few minutes, he looked over and saw her slumped in the chair, breathing fast and heavy, her face drawn on one side. Her blue eyes, wide and full of panic, fixed upon him. She whimpered like a child.

"My God," he said, and he jumped for the phone.

In the hospital, he had sat in the uncomfortable chair and watched her wane, a beautiful picture fading before his eyes. With their gnarled fingers intertwined, he reminisced about their courtship, their wedding day, how divine she had looked in her dress, and how he had made that silly face when they raised their toast because he hated the taste of alcohol. But most importantly, how very lucky he was. He whispered about the birth of their son, and how beautiful she had been while she carried him, and how blessed he was to have spent every one of the last 20,805 days with her as his wife. He told her how much he loved her no less than one hundred times.

Small sighing breaths were the only response from Marie, until they disappeared on that fifth day.

Avery recalled all of this as he stood at the sink and washed the soup dish.

He began the long process of filling baggies with warm water from the tap. It had been a long week — the longest he would ever endure — and he was dog-tired, but it needed to be done. The window over the sink steamed up as he did so. He turned each baggie upside down to ensure the seal wouldn't leak, and then one by one placed them gently into the storage tote by his feet.

The Christmas decorations Marie had wanted him to put up last weekend were now sitting in a pile beside the dining room table. He had only managed to get a single strand of silver tinsel looped along the banister. The light reflected on it like tears.

The tote weighed heavy on his old bones — his cross to bear — as he carried it upstairs.

Aside from a few days here and there when he was away on business, or Marie was visiting her sister, Avery had not slept alone in all the time they'd been married. He wasn't sure he could do it now.

He pulled back the covers and stared at Marie's indentation in the mattress. She always slept in the same position, curled up like a question mark. His arthritic fingers touched the spot where her shape remained, and he sobbed quietly. He slowly removed the baggies from the tote and placed them into the impression of her. From the hook on the bathroom door, he took her bathrobe and covered the baggies, tucking it under each one.

In the dim light of the bedroom, Avery removed his clothing and turned off the bedside lamp. He draped an arm over the warm shape where Marie had once slept, where he felt her now sleeping. He breathed in the smell of soap and sweat and familiarity.

Just before sleep pulled him down, something lightly brushed his tear-streaked cheek. Avery imagined one of Marie's silver strands of hair, decorated in his tears, like tinsel.

ACKNOWLEDGMENTS

Thanks to all of my family and friends. If I know you, I thank you.

Special Thanks to Ken Wood, Nick Contor and Mercedes Yardley and Shock Totem. You guys saw me starting this and still it would have never happened if not for you all.

To Bob Ford for always listening and Chad Lutzke for loving one of these stories enough to message me out of the blue and lay the brick upon which we built an amazing relationship.

Thanks again. To Them. To You. Always and foremost, to YOU.

STORY CREDITS

"The Pass" was originally published in TWISTED DREAMS MAGAZINE, February 2011

"Intruder" was originally published in PSYCHOS, edited by John Skipp in 2012

"Summer Gullet" was originally published in BORDERLANDS 6, edited by Olivia and Tom Monteleone in 2016

"Come Tomorrow" was originally published in DARK TIDES, edited by John J. Questore and Eugene Johnson, in 2019

"Salten" was originally published in 32 WHITE HORSES ON A VERMILLION HILL, edited by Duane Pesice in 2018

"Doodlebug" was originally published in ARTERIAL BLOOM, edited by Mercedes M.Yardley in 2020

"A Fee For Fables" was originally published in ONE OF US: A TRIBUTE TO FRANK MICHAELS ERRINGTON, edited by Kenneth W. Cain in 2020

"Them Iron Eyes Cody Blues" was originally published in ROBBED OF SLEEP STORIES TO STAY UP FOR, edited by Troy Blackford in 2014

"Night Games" was originally published in BLIGHT DIGEST, edited by Ron Earl Phillips, Bracken MacLeod and Jan Kozlowski in 2014

"The Going Rate" was originally published in SPLATTERPUNK FIGHTING BACK, edited by Jack Bantry and Kit Power in 2017

"The Worm Eaters" was originally publsihed in 52 STITCHES, edited by Aaron Polson in 2010

"The Recluse" was originally published in HARDENED HEARTS, edited by Eddie Generous in 2017

"Down By The Ocean" was originally published in SPLATTERPUNK issue #5, edited by Jack Bantry in 2014

"Tinsel" was originally published in SHOCK TOTEM 4.5, edited by K. Allen Wood in 2013

All other stories are original to this collection